Illustrator
Howard Chaney

Editor
Walter Kelly

Editorial Project Manager
Karen J. Goldfluss, M.S. Ed.

Editor in Chief
Sharon Coan, M.S. Ed.

Art Director
Elayne Roberts

Associate Designer
Denise Bauer

Cover Artist
Sue Fullam

Product Manager
Phil Garcia

Imaging
Richard Yslava
Ralph Olmedo, Jr.

Publishers
Rachelle Cracchiolo, M.S. Ed.
Mary Dupuy Smith, M.S. Ed.

FOCUS ON ATHLETES

Author

Cynthia Holzschuher

Teacher Created Materials, Inc.
6421 Industry Way
Westminster, CA 92683
www.teachercreated.com

©1997 Teacher Created Materials, Inc.
Reprinted, 2000
Made in U.S.A.
ISBN-1-55734-499-X

Table of Contents

Introduction

From the dawn of recorded human history, the athlete has been an honored figure in every culture on Earth. Arising out of a basic need for survival, physical skills have become a continually refined and elaborate part of our development as humans. Partly utilitarian and partly sheer joy in the exercise of our powers, athletics have continued to develop through the ages, becoming ritualized celebrations of strength, speed, skill, sportsmanship, and spectacle.

At its best, athletics serve as an idealization of the striving human spirit—seeking to unite body, mind, and aspiration into the noblest of possibilities. Athletes themselves serve as individual beacons—torches to guide us on our continuing journey toward excellence. They light the way, showing us how to practice perseverance, dedication, and concentration, enabling us through competition and cooperation to join a peaceful struggle to better ourselves. Like the butterfly laboring to leave the chrysalis, the athlete is a symbol of the continuing struggle to become something better.

The purpose of *Focus on Athletes* is to examine the lives and achievements of 34 notable athletes from around the world. This study and the activities included in this book are intended to sharpen students' understanding and appreciation for athletics in general and individual sacrifice and accomplishment in particular.

Focus on Athletes will enable you to present fascinating motivational information to students. At their best, the inspiring stories of these men and women will encourage teachers and students to aspire to the highest—to achieve in all areas of human endeavor. The symbolic power of athletics is great, so great that in our language the word *hero* is naturally associated will all great athletes. It is this symbolism which serves to inspire us all—student and teacher alike.

Using the Pages

How you choose to use the pages in this book depends on a number of factors which may include school district curriculum guidelines, learning levels of your students, your teaching style and goals, or the importance of a particular athlete to your current classroom theme. The following descriptions of the book's features are intended to help you get the most from each page.

Sections

Focus on Athletes is divided into nine sections: baseball, basketball, figure skating, football, golf, gymnastics, soccer, tennis, track and field. Choose athletes from the sports that interest you. You can use the chart on pages 5–7 for quick information about the sports, countries, and important achievements of 34 specific athletes.

Biographies

The biographies provided can be read aloud to students, copied for group or individual use, or used as reference.

If you are doing an entire unit on athletes, copy and distribute the biography pages as they are studied. Direct your students to glue each picture to a trading card form (page 4) and add important facts. By the end of the unit, students will have a personal collection of trading cards with summaries of information studied.

You may have your students copy team logos and pennants for display. Encourage them to write letters to leagues, halls of fame, and their favorite teams. Contact your local teams to arrange field trips or classroom visits.

Themes

These pages will complement thematic units on the Olympics, Famous Americans, Values, and Sports.

Suggested Activities and Extensions

At the end of each biography, there are suggestions for activities and for extending the study of the athlete or sport. Choose those ideas which best suit your classroom needs and adapt them to your students' abilities and learning styles. They are appropriate for whole class, small group, or individual use. Check your school or public library for related reading selections.

Student Pages

The student sheets cover a variety of skills and learning levels. Assign the pages that are appropriate for your students and feel free to alter the directions if necessary.

Sport _____

Team _____

_____

_____

_____

_____

Trading Card Form

Use this form to make trading cards for your favorite athletes. Cut the pictures from the biography sheets (or draw your own) and add important facts about the player and team. Cut out the shape below, fold it through the center, and glue the back sides shut.

Picture

Sport

Team

Athletes' Chart

Name	Country/Team	Achievements
Roberto Clemente (1934–1972)	Puerto Rico Pittsburgh Pirates	Humanitarian Over .300 batting average for 13 seasons
Ken Griffey, Jr. (1969–)	United States Seattle Mariners	Two Gold Gloves 1992 All-Star Game MVP
Jackie Robinson (1919–1972)	United States Brooklyn Dodgers	First African American in major leagues
Nolan Ryan (1947–)	United States Texas Rangers	5,714 career strikeouts seven no-hitters won 324 games
Larry Bird (1956–)	United States Boston Celtics	National Basketball Association Most Valuable Player, 1984–1986
Wilt Chamberlain (1936–)	United States Philadelphia 76ers Los Angeles Lakers	100-point game, led the league scoring seven times
Michael Jordan (1963–)	United States Chicago Bulls	Led the NBA in scoring 1986–1993, NBA Most Valuable Player, All-Star MVP, Defensive Player of the Year, 1988
Shaquille O'Neal (1972–)	United States Orlando Magic Los Angeles Lakers	Rookie of the Year
Scott Hamilton (1958–)	United States	Olympic gold medal, 1984
Sonja Henie (1912–1969)	Norway	Three Olympic gold medals, six European titles, 10 world titles
Jayne Torvill (1957–)	England	Nine perfect scores, Olympic gold medal, 1984 Olympic bronze medal, 1994
Christopher Dean (1958–)	England	Nine perfect scores, Olympic gold medal, 1984 Olympic bronze medal, 1994

Athletes' Chart (cont.)

Name	Country/Team	Achievements
Kristi Yamaguchi (1971–)	United States	World Singles Champion, 1991 Olympic gold medal, 1992
Joe Montana (1956–)	United States San Francisco 49ers, Kansas City Chiefs	National Football League All-Pro, All-Star, the "Comeback Kid"
Jerry Rice (1962–)	United States San Francisco 49ers	Pro-Bowl, 1987–1993; 49ers leading receiver
Jim Thorpe (1888–1953)	United States Canton Bulldogs, New York Giants	Two Olympic gold medals, greatest all-around male athlete
Herschel Walker (1962–)	United States New Jersey Generals, Dallas Cowboys, Minnesota Vikings, Philadelphia Eagles	Heisman Trophy, 1985 United States Football League Most Valuable Player
Nancy Lopez (1957–)	United States	Ladies Professional Golf Association Hall of Fame, Player of the Year four times
Jack Nicklaus (1940–)	United States	Professional Golf Association Player of the Year five times, six Masters titles, five PGA Championships, four U.S. Open titles
Tiger Woods (1975–)	United States	Youngest golfer (age 21) to win the Masters Tournament, his first attempt at a "major" tournament as a professional
Nadia Comaneci (1961–)	Romania	Seven perfect 10s and five 1976 medals in the Olympics
Sawao Kato (1946–)	Japan	First gymnast to win gold medals in three successive Olympics, most Olympic gold medals by a male gymnast

Athletes' Chart (cont.)

Name	Country/Team	Achievements
Shannon Miller (1977–)	United States	All-around world champion two times, five medals in the 1992 Olympics
Diego Maradona (1960–)	Argentina Napoli, Barcelona	World Cup Most Valuable Player in 1986, South American Player of the Year in 1979 and 1980
Pelé (1940–)	Brazil Santos, Cosmos	Played on three winning World Cup teams
Steve Zungul (1954–)	Yugoslavia New York, Arrows	MISL Triple Crown, 1980, 1982, 1985; MISL all-time leading scorer
Arthur Ashe (1943–1993)	United States	Davis Cup champion, 1968 Wimbledon champion, 1975
Bjorn Borg (1956–)	Sweden	French Open champion, four years, 1975 Davis Cup champion, Wimbledon champion, 1976–1980
Steffi Graf (1969–)	Germany	Olympic gold medal, Tennis Grand Slam
Martina Navratilova (1956–)	Czechoslovakia, United States	Nine Wimbledon championships, 329 titles in all
Jackie Joyner Kersee (1962–)	United States	1988, 1992 Olympic gold medals in heptathlon, Sullivan Award
Carl Lewis (1961–)	United States	Eight Olympic gold medals: 100 meter, 200 meter, 400 meter relay, long jump
Jesse Owens (1913–1980)	United States	Four Olympic gold medals: 100 meter, 200 meter, 400-meter relay, long jump
Babe Didrikson Zaharias (1914–1956)	United States	Olympic gold medals in hurdles, javelin; silver medal in the high jump; 82 career golf titles

Baseball

Baseball has been America's "national pastime" for almost 140 years. It is based on the English game of "rounders" where players hit a ball, run to bases, and are out if the ball is caught before it hits the ground. In the American colonies, an adaptation of the game called "town ball" was played with similar rules and 20 or more players on a side. These were informal games with different rules, depending on the town or city where the game was being played.

The rules were first written in 1845 by the New York Knickerbockers, an informal group that met twice a week to play baseball and have dinner. Their rules were as follows:

- The bases would be 90 feet apart on a diamond-shaped field.

- The pitcher's mound would be 45 feet from the batter.

- Each team would have a set batting order.

- There would be nine defensive positions: pitcher, catcher, shortstop, first baseman, second baseman, third baseman, and three outfielders.

- Each team got a turn to bat during an inning.

- The first team to score 21 points was the winner. (In 1857 this rule was changed to make the game 9 innings long.)

The National Association of Baseball Players was formed in 1858. It had 22 teams from the New York City area. The first paid admission to a game held at Fashion Race Course on Long Island was 50 cents. As more teams formed, the demand for good players increased. They no longer wanted to be unpaid amateurs. By 1868 some teams had begun to pay their top players.

In 1869 the Cincinnati Red Stockings became the first paid professional team in baseball. In 1876, the National League was formed, and many changes were introduced. Pitchers were allowed to throw overhanded, and batters were allowed three strikes for an out and four balls for a walk. Fans were able to buy refreshments during a game.

From 1887–1947, African Americans were not permitted to play in the major leagues. There were about 75 black players in the pros prior to the segregation ruling of 1887. These men wanted to continue to play, so they formed the Negro National League in 1920. Along with two other leagues, the Eastern Colored League (1923) and the Negro American League (1937), these teams competed and held their own World Series and All-Star games. Eventually, white players, owners, and fans realized that it was a mistake to exclude black players from the major leagues. In 1947, Jackie Robinson became the first major league black player when he signed with the Brooklyn Dodgers.

For more information, write to the following addresses:

- Major League Baseball (American League or National League)
  350 Park Avenue
  New York, NY 10022

- National Baseball Hall of Fame
  Box 590
  Cooperstown, NY 13326

Roberto Clemente

(1934–1972)

Roberto Clemente was born on August 18, 1934, in Carolina, Puerto Rico. His parents worked in the sugar cane fields. For awhile, his father, Melchor, sold meat and worked part-time in construction. Roberto's mother, Luisa, worked in a plantation house. They were hard workers and taught their children the value of an education. His parents hoped that Roberto would become an engineer; however, he soon was recognized as having great athletic ability.

In high school, he played baseball, ran track, and threw the javelin. It became apparent that these other sports helped him get in condition for his first love, baseball. When he was 14 years old, a local businessman, Roberto Marin, watched Roberto playing ball and asked him to join his team, the Sello Rojo Rice softball squad. As a result of that, Roberto was acquired by the Juncos, a Double A amateur team. With Marin's continued help, he signed on with the Santurce Crabbers, another Puerto Rican team owned by a scout for the Brooklyn Dodgers, Pedrin Zorilla.

With each of these teams, Roberto continued to watch, practice, and learn. He accepted an offer to play major league baseball for the Brooklyn Dodgers in 1955. The following season he was the first round draft pick of the Pittsburgh Pirates. Roberto Clemente was now known as a capable right fielder and a strong hitter.

He returned to Puerto Rico after every season. In 1964 he married Vera Zabala. They had three sons. In 1966 Roberto won the Most Valuable Player award, and on May 15, 1967, he had his best game, hitting three home runs and a double. In 1971 Roberto was the World Series MVP. In addition, he holds the record for having the most hits in two consecutive games, 10.

After retirement as a player, Roberto continued to manage Puerto Rican league teams. He was asked to run for mayor of San Juan. Roberto Clemente was killed on December 31, 1972, while on a relief mission to help the earthquake victims of Managua, Nicaragua. His light plane went down in the Atlantic Ocean. On August 6, 1973, he became the first Latin American player to be inducted into the Hall of Fame. His uniform, number 21, was retired by the Pittsburgh Pirates.

Suggested Activities and Extensions

1. Locate Carolina, Puerto Rico, and Managua, Nicaragua, on a map of the world. Determine as closely as possible the latitude and longitude for each place.

2. For more information about Roberto Clemente or current players, write the following address:

   Pittsburgh Pirates
   P.O. Box 7000
   Pittsburgh, Pennsylvania 15212

3. Brainstorm a list of Latin American baseball players (past and present). Sort them by country of origin.

4. Roberto Clemente was also a hero because of his humanitarian work throughout Latin America. At his death, memorial gifts were used to build the *Ciudad Deportiva* (Sports City) where young Puerto Rican boys can develop their athletic abilities. Write a dedication for the facility that tells the contributions Roberto made to his people.

5. Another Puerto Rican athlete of wide fame for his extraordinary skill, good humor, and extensive humanitarian work is golfer Chi Chi Rodriquez. Research his sports accomplishments, background, and present activities. Make a Venn diagram comparing and contrasting Chi Chi Rodriguez and Roberto Clemente.

6. Write three questions you would like to ask Roberto Clemente. Pass them to a friend to answer as Clemente would have.

7. Discuss what can be learned from the life of this man. Consider his success despite adversity, his humanitarianism, his willingness to work, and his natural talent.

8. Think about the important events in Roberto Clemente's life.

   • Write headlines that describe three of those events.

   • Write a news story for one of your headlines.

Related Reading_____

Baseball Tips by Dean Hughes and Tom Hughes. Random Books for Young Readers, 1993.

Pastime by Larry Burke and Paul Ladewski. Smithmark, 1995.

Puerto Rico by Kathleen Thompson. Raintree, 1986.

Roberto Clemente by Peter C. Bjorkman. Chelsea House, 1991.

Roberto Clemente by Thomas W. Gilbert. Chelsea, 1991.

Roberto Clemente by Norman L. Macht. Chelsea House, 1993.

Roberto Clemente: Baseball Legend by Alan West. Millbrook Press, 1993.

Roberto Clemente: Puerto Rican Baseball Player by Tom Gilbert. Chelsea House, 1993.

The Super Book of Baseball by Ron Berler. Sports Illustrated Books for Kids, 1991.

Ken Griffey, Jr.

(1969–)

George Kenneth Griffey, Jr., was born November 21, 1969, in Donora, Pennsylvania, and raised in Cincinnati, Ohio, where his father (Ken senior) was playing baseball for the Cincinnati Reds. Junior was a Little League pitcher, winning all 12 games in his first year.

He starred in baseball and football at Moeller High School in Cincinnati. During his senior year, Junior set school records by batting .478 with seven home runs and 28 RBIs. He stole 13 bases in 28 games. Major league scouts were watching him at every game.

By age 17 Junior was drafted by the Seattle Mariners and assigned to their minor league club in Bellingham, Washington. He had a .313 batting average and hit 14 home runs in only 54 games. The next year his average was .325 with 13 home runs in 75 games.

By 1989 Junior had made it to the major leagues. He was 19 years old and the starting center fielder for the Seattle Mariners. Kenny, Jr., and his father (who joined the Mariners in 1990) were the first father-son team to play for the same team in the history of baseball. During the 1990 season, the Griffeys hit back-to-back home runs.

Ken Griffey, Jr., became the star the Mariners would build around for the future. In 1990, he was voted to the American All-Star team and won a Gold Glove for his work in center field. The 1991 season found Kenny with a .327 batting average and 22 home runs. He drove in 100 runs and won his second straight Gold Glove. In the 1992 All-Star Game he hit a home run and was the game's Most Valuable Player. He was married to his wife, Melissa, in 1992. Their son Trey was born two years later.

By 1994 Junior was the youngest player to have started in five All-Star Games. He has won four Gold Glove Awards. Junior received more All-Star votes than any player in history and won the home run contest at the 1994 All-Star Game with seven round-trippers. He was on his way to topping the single season home run record (61) when play was cut short by the baseball strike. Today, at 26 years of age, Ken Griffey, Jr., is enjoying his wife and family as an established baseball star with an exciting future.

Suggested Activities and Extensions

1. Do you think it would be easy to walk in the footsteps of a famous father? What pressures are on Ken Griffey, Jr., that are not on other young major league players? Discuss.

2. Make a chart of benefits and drawbacks that might follow a team that employed a father-son combination on the athletic field. Don't forget to consider the effects on other players on the team.

3. Read more about these father-son major leaguers: Hal and Brian McRae; Bobby and Barry Bonds; Ray, Bob, and Brett Boone; Randy and Todd Hundley; Sandy, Sandy, Jr., and Roberto Alomar; and Felipe and Moises Alou. Make a chart showing their teams and positions.

4. Ken Griffey, Jr., plays center field. What is his responsibility at this position? Brainstorm a list of other major league center fielders.

5. Research a statistical comparison of the Griffeys' (father and son) lifetime baseball careers. Create a graph or chart showing the following information for each:

Statistics	Ken Griffey, Jr.	Ken Griffey, Sr.
singles		
doubles		
triples		
home runs		
errors		
total games played		

6. For more information about Ken Griffey, Jr., or current players, write to the following address:

    Seattle Mariners
    P.O. Box 4100
    Seattle, Washington 98104

7. Locate Donora, Pennsylvania; Cincinnati, Ohio; and Seattle, Washington, on a map. Do you think Ken, Jr., will remain a player for the Seattle Mariners for his entire career? Explain the pros and cons for Ken (and the Mariners).

Related Reading

Ken Griffey, Jr. by John Rolfe. Bantam, 1995.

Ken Griffey, Jr. by James Rothaus. Childs World, 1991.

Ken Griffey, Jr.: All-Around Star by Barbara Kramer. Lerner Group, 1996.

Ken Griffey, Jr.: The Kid by Howard Reiser. Childrens Press, 1994.

Ken Griffey, Jr., and Ken Griffey, Sr. by Skip Press. Silver Burdett, 1995.

Ken Griffey, Sr., and Ken Griffey, Jr., Father and Son Teammates by Bill Gutman. Millbrook, 1993.

The Seattle Mariners by James R. Rothaus. Creative Education, 1987.

The First Five Years

Here are the Griffeys' box scores for the first five years. Read the charts and answer the questions.

Junior

Year	Games	Batting Average	At Bats	Hits	Home Runs	Runs	RBI
1989	127	.264	455	120	16	61	61
1990	155	.300	597	179	22	91	80
1991	154	.327	548	179	22	76	100
1992	142	.308	565	174	27	83	103
1993	156	.309	582	180	45	113	109

Senior

Year	Games	Batting Average	At Bats	Hits	Home Runs	Runs	RBI
1973	25	.384	86	33	3	19	14
1974	88	.251	227	57	2	24	19
1975	132	.305	463	141	4	95	46
1976	148	.336	562	189	6	111	74
1977	154	.318	585	186	12	117	57

Check the correct answer:	Junior	Senior
1. Who played more games his first season?		
2. Who had the higher batting average his first season?		
3. Who hit more home runs his first season?		
4. Who had more RBI his first season?		

Answer with a number:

1. What was senior's 1976 batting average?   1. _____
2. What was junior's 1991 batting average?   2. _____
3. In what year did junior hit the most home runs?   3. _____
4. In what year did senior have the most RBI?   4. _____
5. How many hits did junior have in 1990?   5. _____
6. In what year did senior play in 154 games?   6. _____

- -

Fold under.

Answers

1. junior   2. senior   3. junior   4. junior
1. .336   2. .327   3. 1993   4. 1976   5. 179   6. 1977

Jackie Robinson

(1919–1972)

Jack Roosevelt Robinson was born in Cairo, Georgia, on January 31, 1919. He was the son of sharecroppers and the grandson of slaves. His father left the family when Jackie was an infant, so his mother moved to Pasadena, California, to find work and a better life for her five children.

In school Jackie excelled in all sports. He was the first person in the history of the University of California to letter in four sports: track, baseball, football, and basketball. He was named a college All-American in football (1941) but had to drop out of school later that year to help earn money for his family. In 1941 he played professional football for the Honolulu Bears, and in 1942 he was drafted into the army.

He was playing baseball for the Kansas City Monarchs, a team in the Negro Leagues, when Branch Rickey, the owner of the Brooklyn Dodgers, asked him to join his team. Rickey felt it was time to "break the color line" in the major leagues. Jackie realized he would face some difficult times but decided he must accept the offer. He married Rachel Isum, his college sweetheart, who provided him with support and a strong family to help.

Some white players said they would not play on a team with a black man, but on opening day of the 1946 minor league season when Jackie had four hits, including a three-run homer, two stolen bases, and scored four times, they changed their minds. As a Dodger, Jackie Robinson was known as an excellent hitter, fielder, and runner. He led the league with 29 stolen bases his first year as a Dodger. In 1947 Jackie Robinson was given the first Rookie of the Year award.

Two years later, he had a .342 batting average with 37 stolen bases. Two other black players, Don Newcombe and Roy Campanella joined the Dodgers. In the years between 1946 and 1952, the team won six National League Championships and one World Series. Jackie Robinson was the National League MVP in 1949 and was elected to the National Baseball Hall of Fame in 1972. His uniform, number 42, has been retired by the Los Angeles Dodgers.

Jackie Robinson was active in civil rights after he retired from baseball. He was adviser to Governor Nelson Rockefeller of New York and Democratic presidential candidate Lyndon Johnson. He will always be remembered for his courage in breaking the color line in the major leagues. Jackie Robinson died at the age of 53 of complications from diabetes.

14

Suggested Activities and Extensions

1. Jackie Robinson paved the way for other minority players to enter the major leagues. What do you suppose they would like to say to him if they could meet him today? Write a dialogue between a young rookie of today meeting Robinson and discussing the changes that have taken place in baseball and in America itself.

2. For more information about Jackie Robinson or current players, write to the following address:
    > Los Angeles Dodgers
    > 1000 Elysian Park Avenue
    > Los Angeles, California 90012

3. Discuss or write about how you would have felt being Jackie Robinson in 1946. What decision would you have made about "breaking the color line"? Do you think it was his responsibility to do this in order to help other minorities? Explain.

4. Read more about Don Newcombe and Roy Campanella. Summarize the information on trading card forms (page 4).

5. Jackie Robinson played on the major league All-Star team every year from 1949 to 1954. Write a research paper about last year's All-Star game. Where was it held? Who were the players on each team? What were their positions? Who were the managers? What was the final score? What important plays were made?

6. Write to the University of California at Los Angeles (UCLA) for information about Jackie Robinson's athletic accomplishments during his brief stay at that school. Research other black athletes who followed his footsteps at that university.

7. Research the baseball career of Satchel Paige, another black baseball player of extraordinary accomplishment and longevity. Compile a list of his statistics—number of years playing, wins and losses as a pitcher, number of major league starts, etc.

8. Interview someone old enough to have seen Jackie Robinson play baseball. Ask questions about Robinson's abilities on the field, his effect on other players, his effect on the fans, and his effect on the news of the time. Was his influence felt beyond the baseball field? Record your interview on tape if it is all right with the person being interviewed; then play the interview back to the class.

Related Reading

All-Time Great World Series by Andrew Gutelle. Grosset and Dunlap, 1994.

In the Year of the Boar and Jackie Robinson by Bette Bao Lord. Harper and Row, 1987.

Jackie Robinson by Manfred Weidhorn. Simon & Schuster, 1992.

Jackie Robinson: Baseball's Civil Rights Legend by Karen M. Coombs. Enslow Publications, 1997.

Leagues Apart by Lawrence S. Ritter. Morrow Junior Books, 1995.

Shadow Ball by Geoffrey C. Ward. Knopf, 1994.

The Story of Negro League Baseball by William Brashler. Ticknor and Fields, 1994.

Teammates by Paul Bacon. Harcourt, Brace, Jovanovich, 1990.

Take Me Out to the Ball Game by Jack Norworth. Four Winds Press, 1993 (illustrations of 1947 Ebbets Field).

Computing a Batting Average

To compute Jackie Robinson's batting averages, you must divide the number of his hits by the number of his official at bats. You may want to use a calculator.

Season	Hits	At Bats	Batting Average
1947	175	590	
1948	170	574	
1949	203	593	
1950	170	518	
1951	185	548	
1952	157	510	
1953	159	484	
1954	120	386	
1955	81	317	
1956	98	357	

Plot the yearly averages on this line graph.

Average										
.350										
.340										
.330										
.320										
.310										
.300										
.290										
.280										
.270										
.260										
.250										
Season	'47	'48	'49	'50	'51	'52	'53	'54	'55	'56

Bonus: Attend a baseball game, choose a player, and compute his or her batting average for the entire game.

- -

Fold under.

Answers:

1947—.297, 1948—.296, 1949—.342, 1950—.328, 1951—.338, 1952—.308, 1953—.329, 1954—.311, 1955—.256, 1956—.275.

Nolan Ryan

(1947–)

Lynn Nolan Ryan was born in Refugio, Texas, on January 31, 1947. His family moved to Alvin, Texas, where Nolan's father was an oil plant supervisor. As a child, Nolan played Little League baseball and strengthened his arm by rolling and throwing newspapers for his paper route. He was to become the fastest pitcher in the history of baseball.

In high school Ryan won 20 games and lost only four. Before graduation, he was spotted by Red Murff, a scout for the New York Mets, and was drafted by them in the eighth round in 1965. He spent two years in the minor leagues. In 1968, Nolan Ryan entered the majors as a relief pitcher. He could throw very fast, but because his pitching could be wild, he was not ready to be a starter. He was traded to the American League's California Angels.

There he met coaches Jimmy Reese and Tom Morgan, who helped him to control his pitching. In his first three seasons in California, Ryan won 62 games. In 1973 he pitched two no-hitters and struck out 383 batters. By 1979 as a free agent, Nolan Ryan eagerly accepted the opportunity to play for the Houston Astros. He was happy to be near his boyhood home of Alvin, Texas.

Ryan became a strong power pitcher who broke Sandy Koufax's record of four career no-hitters by throwing his fifth no-hitter in 1981. By 1991 Ryan had pitched two more for a grand total of seven career no-hitters, his last when he was 44 years old, a remarkable physical accomplishment. While in Houston, he broke Walter Johnson's record for the most career strikeouts (3,509). In 1988 Nolan joined the Texas Ranger organization and achieved his 5,000th career strikeout at the age of 44. Most people believe that the "Ryan Express" was the greatest pitcher of all time, having a fast ball timed at 100.9 miles per hour, as well as an excellent curve ball and change-up. He played on eight All-Star teams.

Nolan Ryan retired from baseball in 1993 at the age of 46.

Suggested Activities and Extensions

1. Share the poem "Casey at the Bat" by Ernest Lawrence Thayer. The next to last verse reads as follows:

   The sneer has fled from Casey's lip, his teeth are clenched in hate;

   He pounds with cruel violence his bat upon the plate.

   And now the pitcher holds the ball, and now he lets it go,

   And now the air is shattered by the force of Casey's blow.

Individually or with partners, try composing a verse in the same rhythm and rhyme scheme, describing the pitcher as Nolan Ryan. Make sure the action fits the concluding stanza. An example might read something like the following:

   So Casey faces Ryan now, who stands upon the mound

   And digs his spikes with all his might, so deep into the ground.

   He hurls the ball so hard and fast, with blinding, blazing speed

   That Casey thinks he's swinging at a watermelon seed.

2. Talk to a trainer or coach about conditioning for pitchers.

3. Invite someone to your classroom to discuss sports medicine and the kinds of injuries that are common to baseball players, particularly pitchers.

4. Do you believe the pitcher is the most important player on the team? Debate opposing positions.

5. Organize a class baseball game and give everyone a chance to practice throwing at a target to understand pitching control.

6. Research information about baseball equipment, especially that used by catchers. Make a list of famous catchers: Johnny Bench, Yogi Berra, etc. Learn how the catcher and pitcher work together.

7. Explain the following plays and draw diagrams of a baseball field, using stick figures to illustrate each play:

   • the intentional walk (How does a catcher signal the pitcher for this?)

   • the bunt (Show how to hold the bat.)

   • the hit-and-run play

   • the steal (Show and tell when the base runner should leave the base.)

   • the slide (Explain the head-first and feet-first slides.)

8. Take the class out to a baseball diamond on the school playground. Let two students illustrate the movements described in the diagrams from number seven. Let one other student show how a pitcher would most likely defend against the bunt, the hit-and-run, and the steal.

Related Reading

Nolan Ryan by John Rolfe. Little Brown, 1992.

Standard Pitches

Fast Ball

The ball is held with the second and third fingers resting on the seams. The thumb is underneath. When delivering the ball, the pitcher snaps his wrist and elbow forward, making the ball spin. The ball is thrown with all the speed the pitcher can manage. It may veer slightly to the left or right or up or down. Nolan Ryan's fast ball was clocked at 100.9 miles per hour, the fastest in the history of baseball.

Curve

Most pitchers grip the ball across the seams. The thumb is underneath. The pitcher must jerk his hand down in front of his body as he lets go of the ball. The release is what makes the ball spin and curve. This pitch breaks down and away from the batter. It must be kept low and on the corners of home plate.

Change-Up (sometimes called "off speed")

A pitcher must also be able to change the speed of his pitches. This upsets the batters timing when thrown together with several fast balls. The pitcher grips the ball loosely in the palm of his hand. There is no spin on the ball when it is released. To be effective, the delivery must look the same as a fast ball in order to fool the batter.

Which Is Which?

  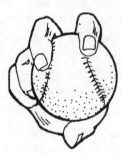

Pitching Strategy

The pitcher's goal is to make the batter swing and miss. His greatest strength is in his ability to mix pitches, changing the character and speed of each one in order to confuse the batter.

The count is one factor that determines what kind of pitch is thrown. If there are no balls but two strikes, the pitch should be different than if there are two balls and no strikes. If the count favors the pitcher, he can afford to waste a pitch by throwing outside the strike zone. The number of outs, the score, and whether there are men on base are other factors to be considered when planning a pitching strategy.

Answer the following:

1. What factors make a great pitcher? _____

   _____

2. What must a pitcher consider when facing a batter? _____

   _____

Basketball

The game of basketball was invented in December 1891 by Dr. James Naismith, a physical education teacher at the Young Men's Christian Association Training School in Springfield, Massachusetts.

The original game used a round ball and two peach baskets as goals. Dr. Naismith nailed the baskets to the balcony at each end of the gym. He made these rules:

- There were nine players on each side.

- The ball could be thrown or batted in either direction, but not hit with the fist.

- All bodily contact was considered a foul.

- A player left the game after two fouls, and he could not be substituted for until the other team had made a goal.

- If either team committed three consecutive fouls, the other team was awarded a goal.

- A game had two 15-minute halves. There could be sudden-death overtime if both captains agreed.

These changes came later: The game periods were lengthened to two 20 minute halves in 1893–1894, and the 15-foot free throw was introduced in the 1895–1896 season. In the 1896–1897 season the value of a field goal was set at two points. The number of players was set at five per team during the next season. Five minute overtimes replaced the sudden-death overtime in 1907–1908. Dribbling did not become part of the game until 1929. In the 1930s other changes were made to speed up the game. The 10-second rule (requiring the offensive team to bring the ball past midcourt in 10 seconds) was begun in 1933, and the center jump after every basket was eliminated in 1938.

The first professional game was played in Trenton, New Jersey, in 1896. The first professional players were organized as teams and toured the country, competing against local teams for a share of the ticket sales. The National Basketball League was formed in 1937, and the Basketball Association of America in 1946. In 1949 the two leagues combined to form the National Basketball Association. Today the NBA is made up of 27 teams, 14 in the Eastern Conference and 13 in the Western Conference.

Women began playing basketball very early. The first women's college team was organized at Smith College in 1893. They played by men's rules until 1899 when several rules were changed to control rough play. Women's professional basketball teams toured the United States from 1936–1974, playing any local teams that would accept their challenge. Recently, more new teams have appeared.

For more information contact the following sources:

- National Basketball Association Olympic Tower 645 Fifth Avenue, New York, New York 10022

- Naismith Memorial Basketball Hall of Fame 1150 West Columbus Avenue, Springfield, Massachusetts 01105

Larry Bird

(1956–)

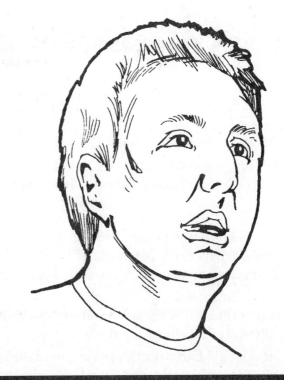

Larry Joe Bird was born December 7, 1956, in French Lick, Indiana. There were six children in the Bird family. Joe Bird, Larry's father, worked in a piano factory, and his mother, Georgia, was a restaurant and factory worker. Larry got his first basketball for Christmas when he was just four years old.

His high school coach remembers Larry as a hard worker: "He didn't have a car, or much money, so he spent his time at basketball." By the time he was a senior at Springs Valley High School, Larry had grown to six feet seven inches tall and averaged 30 points and 20 rebounds a game. He had more than 200 college scholarship offers on graduation, but Larry decided to stay close to home and in the fall of 1974 enrolled at the University of Indiana. He felt uncomfortable at the university, which was much larger than his entire hometown, and he quit after only 24 days. He returned to French Lick and got a job driving a garbage truck.

Bill Hodges, the coach at Indiana State University, visited Larry at his home in French Lick. He offered Larry a scholarship and talked with him about his future. Hodges was successful, for in three years at Indiana State University, Larry averaged 30.3 points per game and set 14 school records. In 1979 he led the team to the National Collegiate Athletic Association (NCAA) finals. He was chosen College Player of the Year for the 1978–1979 season.

Larry joined the Boston Celtics and was voted Rookie of the Year in 1980. The Celtics won National Basketball Association (NBA) titles in 1981, 1984, and 1986. Larry was the Most Valuable Player for the NBA's regular season for three consecutive years, 1984–1986. He was known as one of the hardest workers in professional basketball, able to dribble and shoot with both hands and hit three-pointers as well as layups.

Though he continued to play very well, Larry was bothered by bone spurs in his heels and a ruptured disk in his back. In 1988 a life-size statue of him was placed in the New England Sports Museum. In French Lick, a street is named in his honor. Larry retired from basketball after fulfilling his commitment to play on the United States "dream team" in the 1992 Barcelona Olympics.

Suggested Activities and Extensions

1. For more information about Larry Bird or current players, write to the following address:

   Boston Celtics
   151 Merrimac Street, 5th Floor
   Boston, Massachusetts 02114

2. Larry Bird is one of only five men in NBA history to score 20,000 points. If he played seven seasons, how many points did he average each season? If there are 82 games per season, what is the average number of points scored per game?

3. Larry Bird was a guard in high school and a forward in the pros. What are the differences in the two positions? What are the advantages and disadvantages to being a good all-round player as opposed to excelling in just one area of play?

4. How would Larry Bird's life have been different if he had stayed in French Lick driving a garbage truck after leaving the University of Indiana? Why is it important to have long-range goals? Discuss.

5. It has been said that Larry Bird's greatest talent may be his desire to work. How can a willingness to work overcome a lack of natural ability? Apply this concept to your life.

6. Larry Bird calls himself "the hick from French Lick." He has remained a private person despite his celebrity. How do you think you would respond to the publicity and popularity of being a superstar athlete? What would be good and bad about the attention?

7. Research Larry Bird's free-throw record. How would this record have affected his overall scoring average?

8. Did Larry Bird ever foul out of a pro game? How many times?

9. College and professional basketball players are often taught to foul an opponent deliberately. Why is this so, and under what circumstances does it take place?

10. Write an explanation of what you think has been the greatest change in the game of basketball since Dr. Naismith's original rules of the game were developed in 1891. (You may refresh your memory of those rules by referring to page 20.)

11. Using stick figures to illustrate, explain "goal tending" and what the scoring result should be.

    - Why does this rarely occur in school games?
    - Why is this a difficult play for the referees to call?

12. One of Larry Bird's most difficult moves to defend against was the "fall-away shot." Explain what a fall-away shot is and illustrate with a stick-figure diagram.

Related Reading

Boston Celtics by Michael E. Goodman. Creative Education, 1993.
Larry Bird by Sean Dolan. Chelsea House, 1995.
Larry Bird by Matthew Newman. Crestwood House, 1986.
Team U.S.A. by Devra Speregen. Scholastic, 1992.

Motivation and Success

Motivation and the willingness to work hard are important traits of professional athletes in any sport. Larry Bird became a fine all-around basketball player after years of practice. His determination led him to greatness.

1. What do you think motivates an athlete like Larry Bird?

   _____

   _____

   _____

   _____

2. At one point, Larry had dropped out of college and was driving a garbage truck. Indiana State University basketball coach Bill Hodges helped him understand the importance of an education and persuaded him to give college another try. What do you think Larry Bird would say to Bill Hodges today?

   _____

   _____

   _____

   _____

3. In life, people are motivated by many things—personal need for success, desire for money, peer pressure, verbal praise, etc. What motivates you to excellence?

   _____

   _____

   _____

   _____

4. In what area of your life are you the most successful?

   _____

   _____

   _____

5. How might that success help you in the future?

   _____

   _____

   _____

   _____

Wilt Chamberlain

(1936–)

Wilton Norman Chamberlain was born in Philadelphia, Pennsylvania, August 21, 1936. There were eleven children in his family. His father was a welder, and his mother worked as a maid. Wilt was six feet ten inches tall by age 15, so basketball was a natural choice for him. He averaged 36.3 points per game in three years at Overbrook High School in Philadelphia. In one game he scored 90 points. On graduation, he had 200 offers for college scholarships.

Wilt decided to attend the University of Kansas, where he played basketball and participated in track. In college, at seven feet one inch tall, he was nicknamed "Wilt the Stilt" and "The Big Dipper." He dropped out of college after three years to play for the Harlem Globetrotters. Wilt signed with the Philadelphia Warriors and was named National Basketball Association (NBA) Rookie of the Year in 1960. He led the NBA in scoring for seven straight years and was the Most Valuable Player four times through 1973.

On March 2, 1962, in Hershey, Pennsylvania, Wilt scored 100 points (and 20 rebounds) against the New York Knicks. That remains the highest total score ever in an NBA game by a single player. In the 1961–1962 season he averaged 50.4 points per game.

He joined the Philadelphia 76ers at the end of the 1964–1965 season. During the 1966–1967 season under coach Alex Hannum, the 76ers were the most talented team in the NBA. When Coach Hannum resigned, Wilt asked to be traded. He joined the Los Angeles Lakers in 1968–1969.

Wilt proved to be the great center the Lakers needed to complete a winning team. Unfortunately, Wilt's right knee gave way during the ninth game of the 1969–1970 season. He required immediate surgery but accepted the challenge of rehabilitation and by March had met his goal of returning for the playoffs. The Lakers were defeated by the Knicks in a seven-game series. The Lakers under Coach Bill Sharman finally won their first championship in 1971–1972. Chamberlain was named the NBA Finals' Most Valuable Player.

Wilt's play accounts for more than 75% of all the highest scoring performances during his 33-year career. His accomplishments are amazing, including 31,419 career points and 23,924 rebounds. He is the greatest NBA center of all time.

Suggested Activities and Extensions

1. Wilt Chamberlain played 14 seasons in the NBA. He scored a total of 31,419 points. How many points did he average per season? If there are 82 games per season, what is the average number of points scored per game?

2. Wilt Chamberlain's highest number of free throws (28) in a game occurred in 1962. Take your class to the gym for a free-throw contest. Keep track of the number of throws attempted and scored by each player. Compute each student's free-throw average. Estimate how many tries one of your students would need to hit 28 free throws.

3. For more information about Wilt Chamberlain or current players, write to the following address:

   > Los Angeles Lakers
   > Great Western Forum
   > 3900 West Manchester Blvd.
   > Inglewood, California 90396

4. Read more about Abe Saperstein and the Harlem Globetrotters. The all-black team was founded in 1929 and was known for its comic style of play. They traveled around the world, often drawing larger crowds than the NBA.

5. In retirement, Wilt has played and coached professional volleyball. Which of his basketball skills would transfer to the sport of volleyball? How could his basketball experience help him become a good coach?

6. Wilt Chamberlain was such a superb athlete that some observers felt he could have succeeded as a professional in any sport, including boxing. Check up on this possibility and write a brief explanation of why many people have thought this.

7. Kareem Abdul-Jabbar became a center for the Los Angeles Lakers after Wilt Chamberlain. His accomplishments have also been record-setting for the team and for the NBA. Compare the records of the two men in a chart such as the following:

Statistics	Chamberlain	Jabbar
Total Field Goals		
Total Free Throws		
Percentage Field Goals		
Percentage Free Throws		
Total Points Scored		
Total Games Played		

Related Reading _____

Los Angeles Lakers by Michael E. Goodman. Creative Education, 1993.
Volleyball for Boys and Girls by Bill Gutman. Grey Castle Press, 1990.
Wilt Chamberlain by Ron Frankl. Chelsea House, 1994.

The 100-Point Game

Compute the scores in each problem. A field goal is worth two points and a free throw, one.

Cross out the sentences that are not needed to work the problem.

1. Wilt played his highest scoring game for the Philadelphia Warriors March 2, 1962. He had seven field goals and nine free throws in the first quarter. How many points had he scored? _____

2. Wilt almost never fouled out of a game. He made seven field goals and four free throws in the second quarter. How many points did he score? _____

3. Wilt remained hot during the third quarter of the game, scoring 10 field goals and eight free throws. The Warriors were ahead 125–106. How many points did Wilt score in the third quarter? _____

4. Wilt's play was extraordinary that night. What is the total number of points he scored in the first three quarters of the game? _____

5. Wilt's previous record for the most points scored in a game was 78. By the end of the third quarter, he knew he had a chance to break the record. How many points did he need? _____

6. In the fourth quarter, nothing the Knicks tried would stop Wilt. He scored 11 field goals and seven free throws. How many points did he score in the fourth quarter? _____

7. There were 42 seconds left in the fourth quarter. How many points had Wilt scored so far in the game? How many points did he need to reach 100? _____

The fans cheered when Wilt made his final basket. They had watched the greatest scoring exhibition in basketball history. The final score was 169–147.

Complete this chart using the information from the problem.

Period	Field Goals	Free Throws
1st quarter		
2nd quarter		
3rd quarter		
4th quarter		
Totals		

Fold under.

Answers:

			field goals	free throws
1. 23	5. 10		7	9
2. 18	6. 29		7	4
3. 28	7. 2		10	8
4. 69			12	7
		Total	**36**	**28**

Michael Jordan

(1963–)

Michael Jeffery Jordan was born February 17, 1963, in Wallace, North Carolina. He was the youngest son born to parents James and Dolores. Before high school, baseball was Michael's favorite sport. He played basketball against his brother Larry in the backyard of the family home.

Michael was cut from the Laney High School varsity basketball team in his sophomore year. Even though he was very athletic, Michael realized he had to work hard to build his basketball skills. His high school coach, Clifton Herring, arranged for him to attend the Five-Star Basketball Camp in Pittsburgh, Pennsylvania. At the camp, Michael was seen by college recruiters and was offered a scholarship to the University of North Carolina.

At UNC he soon became known for making end-of-the-game winning plays. Jordan was named *The Sporting News* College Player of the Year in 1982 and 1983, and in 1984 he received the John R. Wooden Award as the top college player. Jordan led the U.S. basketball team to an Olympic gold medal in 1984 and turned pro after his junior year in college. He signed a multiyear contract with the Chicago Bulls.

As a rookie, Michael Jordan proved to have amazing ability. The crowds loved him. In 1985 he was named Rookie of the Year and started in the All-Star Game. He led his team in points, assists, rebounds, and steals. During the 1986–1987 season, Michael scored at least 40 points in nine straight games. After the 1987 playoffs, he became the first player to be named the NBA's Most Valuable Player and the Defensive Player of the Year in one season.

Against the Cleveland Cavaliers in 1988, Jordan became the first player to score 50 or more points in consecutive playoff games. He scored 226 points during that five-game series. The next season he achieved a total of 10,000 career points. Michael Jordan was the NBA's top scorer for the fifth straight year in the 1990–1991 season, but he continued to work to improve his skill and increase his endurance. He made an extra effort to pass the ball to his teammates and shoot less himself.

The Bulls won 61 games in the 1990–1991 season and swept their finals with the Pistons. They won their first ever NBA title with Jordan averaging 31.2 points, 12.4 assists, and 6.6 rebounds in the finals. The Bulls continued as NBA champs for the next two years. On October 6, 1993, Michael Jordan announced his retirement from basketball. In the spring of 1994, he played minor league baseball with the Birmingham Barons but returned to the Bulls by March 1995.

Suggested Activities and Extensions

1. Brainstorm a list of commercials and products that have a connection to Michael Jordan. Be sure your students understand the huge sums of money that athletes earn from these endorsements. Are you more (or less) likely to buy a product advertised by an athlete? Encourage them to become aware of athletes in commercials. Graph the number of students who have owned Air Jordan shoes or clothing. If appropriate, role-play some of Michael Jordan's commercials.

2. Michael Jordan's father said, "Michael set goals and worked hard to achieve them. He was never one who thought he could get by without working." How important are goal setting and hard work to you? How would Michael Jordan's life have been different without his work ethic and competitive spirit?

3. For more information about Michael Jordan or current players, write to the following address:

   Chicago Bulls
   1 Magnificent Mile
   980 N. Michigan Ave., Suite 1600
   Chicago, Illinois 60611

4. Read more about the U.S. basketball "dream team" in the 1992 Olympics. Who are they? What did they accomplish? Why were NBA players allowed to compete?

5. Look for articles about Michael Jordan in the sports section of the daily newspaper or magazines. Write five questions you would ask Jordan if you were interviewing him.

6. Michael Jordan briefly tried playing baseball with the Chicago White Sox minor league team. Look for additional information about his baseball achievements. What other great athletes have excelled at more than one sport?

7. Read about the scientific basis for the "hang time" Jordan achieves with his spectacular jumps. The total time in the air is probably less than a second; however, his body control gives the illusion that he is able to defy gravity.

8. Michael Jordan attended the University of North Carolina. Research other famous basketball players who went to that school to play the game under that school's celebrated coach. Write a letter to the athletic department at UNC, asking for information about their basketball program.

Related Reading

Airborne by Jesse Kornbluth. Macmillan, 1995.
Basketball Skywalker by Thomas R. Raber. Lerner Group, 1997.
Chicago Bulls by Michael E. Goodman. Creative Education, 1993.
Jordan by Dennis P. Eichorn. Turman, 1987.
A Life Above the Rim by Robert Lipsyte. HarperC Children's Books, 1994.
Michael Jordan by Chip Lovitt. Scholastic, 1991.
Science and Sports by Robert Gardner. F. Watts, 1988.
Team U.S.A. by Devra Speregen. Scholastic, 1992.

Award Ceremony

Michael Jordan has won many basketball awards. Choose one of them and research what he did to win. Pretend you will be the presenter at the awards ceremony. Write a speech for yourself and an acceptance speech that Jordan might say. Design the award.

Presenter	Michael Jordan

Award

Shaquille O'Neal

(1972–)

Shaquille Rashaun O'Neal was born March 6, 1972, in Newark, New Jersey. His name means "little warrior" in the Islamic language. He has two younger sisters and a brother. Shaquille's father was a sergeant in the U.S. Army, and when Shaq was 10, the family went to live on a military base in West Germany. Both of his parents were big, so it was not surprising that Shaq had grown to seven feet tall by age 15.

He remembers that it was difficult being so tall as a teenager. None of the stores had clothes that fit him. In school, he was teased because of his name and his size, but Shaq was raised by strict parents who taught him to respect himself and others. He became involved in sports at the army base to keep out of trouble and soon realized that playing basketball was a way to be proud of his size. He determined to work hard and make basketball his ticket to a wonderful life.

He met Coach Dale Brown from Louisiana State University at a basketball clinic on the army base in Germany. Brown was looking for potential student athletes for LSU. O'Neal knew that hard work would make him a complete player by the time he was college age. Two years after he returned to the United States, Shaquille O'Neal was the most sought-after college basketball recruit. He chose to attend Louisiana State University because of his long friendship with Coach Brown.

In three years at LSU, Shaq O'Neal averaged 21.6 points and 13.5 rebounds a game. He was a two-time All-American and received a lot of attention from the press. His face appeared on television and magazine covers. In 1992 he left college to join the Orlando Magic. He signed the biggest contract in the history of team sports.

He was wealthy. Shaquille O'Neal bought a house in Orlando, several cars, a diamond ring, and a leather coat. He used some of his money to help his family. He set up a foundation called "Athletes and Entertainers for Kids" and gave a Thanksgiving dinner to 300 homeless people in Orlando. Everywhere he went, people were impressed with his generosity, maturity, and humility.

Recently, Shaquille O'Neal has joined The Los Angeles Lakers but has not let money and success change him as a person. He is still close to his parents and enjoys sharing his money and time with the less fortunate. He continues to be eager to learn and willing to work. He is quick, strong, and an excellent shot. Win or lose, he is an exciting player to watch and destined to become an NBA legend.

Suggested Activities and Extensions

1. For more information about Shaquille O'Neal or current players, write to the following address:

   Los Angeles Lakers
   Great Western Forum
   3900 West Manchester Blvd.
   Inglewood, CA 90396

2. Brainstorm a list of commercials and products that have featured Shaq. Add them to your list of Michael Jordan endorsements. Which products do your students prefer? Are their choices based on the personality of the athlete or the quality of the product?

3. Shaquille O'Neal uses his money to help other people and his family. What would you do with all that money? Make lists of things you would buy yourself and others. Do you think having a lot of money would change you? Explain.

4. How do you think O'Neal's life was changed by living on a military base in a foreign country? What might have happened if he had remained in Newark, New Jersey? Which setting gave him the better chance for a successful future?

5. What would be good (and bad) about being seven feet one inch tall? What do you think is a perfect height? Explain.

6. Challenge your students to go "shopping for Shaq." Look in your local stores for size 20 shoes. Trace around the bottom of one and compare it to the size of your students' feet. Survey the cost of a complete set of clothes for a person the size of Shaquille O'Neal:

   shirt: _____   shoes:_____

   pants: _____   jacket: _____

   socks: _____   total: _____

8. His mother and father were disappointed when Shaq dropped out of LSU. They believe that education is very important. Do you think he will ever return and finish his degree? Debate the pros and cons of leaving college to join the NBA. What would you have done? Explain.

9. What do you think the future holds for Shaquille O'Neal? Will he complete his college degree? Will he marry and start a family? Will he be injured and change careers?

   Write an article for a sports magazine, telling where O'Neal will be and what he will be doing 10 years from now.

Related Reading_____

Orlando Magic by Richard Rambeck. Creative Education, 1993.
Shaquille O'Neal by Neil Cohen. Bantam, 1993.
Shaquille O'Neal by Edward Tallman. Maxwell Macmillan, 1994.
Sports Great Shaquille O'Neal by Michael Sullivan. Enslow, 1995.

Figure Skating

The earliest known reference to skating for pleasure was in 1175 when people in London, England, "skated" on polished animal bones attached to their boots. They used sticks to push themselves along. The first skates with iron blades appeared in the Netherlands in the 1200s or 1300s. Because the iron blades were stronger than bone, skaters no longer needed sticks.

Originally, skaters performed rigid routines, tracing patterns on the ice. An American named Jackson Haines created a single unit skate with the blade screwed into the sole. He was the first to add ballet, music, and colorful costumes to the sport. He toured Europe in 1864 to introduce his style of skating to the world. Skating became popular in North America, and the first covered rinks were built in the 1850s. Louis Rubinstein of Montreal, Canada, was the first great figure skater of North America. He won the Canadian championship for 12 years in a row, 1878–1889. Figure skating became an Olympic event in 1908.

Skating competitions have similar rules for men's and women's divisions. The performers skate a technical program of two minutes and 40 seconds and a free-skating program four minutes long for women, and four and one-half minutes long for men. In the technical program, there are eight required moves—three jumps, three spins, and two footwork moves. In the free skate program, the skaters display their artistic and technical skills with original choreography. Skaters are judged on technical merit and artistic impression for both programs. The free skate counts for two-thirds, and the technical program one-third of the skater's total score.

Pair skating began in Vienna, Austria, in the 1800s. The partners perform dangerous throws and lifts. The rules and scoring are similar to singles skating. The required elements include synchronized solo spins, side-by-side jumps, and overhead lifts and throws. Ice dancing is more musical and stylish than athletic. It became an Olympic sport in 1976. In ice dancing, the man is not allowed to lift the woman above his head. The competition has four parts—a two-minute original dance, a four-minute free dance, and two compulsory dances. The free dance is the most important, counting for 50 percent of the final score. In Canada there are two other forms of popular figure skating competition—fours skating, which is similar to pairs but with two men and two women; and precision skating for teams of 12 or more skaters.

Fifty countries belong to the International Skating Union (ISU), which supervises competitions at the junior world and world championships, European championships and the Winter Olympics. Each country also has competitions at the national level. The United States Figure Skating Association sponsors competitions at eight different skill levels.

For more information write to the following address:

> U.S. Figure Skating Association/Figure Skating Hall of Fame and Museum
> 20 First Street
> Colorado Springs, Colorado 80906.

Scott Hamilton

(1958–)

Scott Hamilton was born August 28, 1958, in Toledo, Ohio. He was adopted at six weeks of age by Ernie and Dorothy Hamilton, two college professors from nearby Bowling Green. For no apparent reason, Scott stopped growing at age two. His parents were very concerned and took him to several doctors, seeking advice. One doctor thought Scott had food allergies, and one diagnosed cystic fibrosis, a serious lung disease. Finally, his condition was correctly diagnosed as Schwachmann's syndrome. The boy was unable to absorb the nutrients in food through his intestines. His growth would be stunted forever. He had to eat through a feeding tube.

His older sister, Susan, was instrumental in getting the young Scott involved in figure skating. A year after he began skating, his doctor declared him to be healthy! It seemed that the exercise and cold temperatures at the rink had cured his illness.

With this good news, Hamilton began working harder than ever on his skating. He spent hours working out with his coach, Don Laws, and competed in the 1980 Winter Olympics at Lake Placid. He won his first national title in 1981 and became the first American skater since Hayes Jenkins (1953) to capture the world championship.

When Scott Hamilton competed, skaters had to do three figures chosen by judges at random from 41 patterns. These were called the *school figures*. Scott was best suited for the free skating program. He was able to make the most difficult jumps and spins look easy. In 1984 at Sarajevo he became the first U.S. male skater since David Jenkins (1960) to win a gold medal at the Winter Olympics.

After winning national, world, and Olympic titles, Scott Hamilton toured with Ice Capades and Stars on Ice. He is currently a sports commentator for Olympic figure skating events and still skates on tour.

Suggested Activities and Extensions

1. Scott Hamilton won a gold medal at the Winter Olympics in Sarajevo (1984). Where will the next Winter Olympics be held? Read more about the Olympics and make a list of the winter sports. Add to the list a chart of the other male skaters who have won medals (gold, silver, and bronze) in the events Hamilton entered. Let the list extend from the beginning of Olympic figure skating to the present.

2. Do you think it is likely that Scott Hamilton's health problems were resolved by skating alone? How would that idea effect his commitment to his sport? In general, what are the health benefits of a regular exercise program?

3. Scott Hamilton works as a television commentator at many figure skating events. What kind of information would he need to know before the broadcasts? What questions could he ask the skaters? Learn more about Dick Button, another famous skater who now does skating commentary.

4. If possible, plan a field trip so that your class can try ice skating. Try to arrange for a demonstration by an employee of the rink. Examine the construction of skates.

5. Even though he was small and sickly, Scott Hamilton determined to excel in his sport. He has built a successful career. What other well known figures in sports and/or public life have overcome physical handicaps or weaknesses to become prominent and successful? Design a poster or display featuring the facts about such figures. Discuss the importance of determination and strength of character as a means to achievement. Do your students have personal goals for the future? Be sure they understand that their present talents may lead to future success.

6. Research the design differences between figure skates, hockey skates, and racing skates. Prepare a chart with diagrams showing those distinctions.

7. Are there any special dietary and/or exercise requirements for professional skaters? Research this and prepare a report containing your recommendations.

8. Interview a skating instuctor or coach at a local rink. Seek answers to the following:

   - How much is the average cost of lessons per hour for figure skating?

   - How many hours per day must the average student practice who hopes to become a top amateur or professional?

   - Should talented young children be sent away from home to study with a professional teacher?

   - What are the most important competition events for aspiring young figure skaters to enter?

Related Reading _____

Great Skates by Laura Hilgers. Little, Brown, 1991.
Ice Skating by Tom Wood. Watts, 1990.
The Olympic Games by Theodore Knight. Lucent, 1991.
Skating by Donna Bailey. Raintree, 1990.

The Physics of Skating

Newton's First Law of Motion—*A body at rest or in motion will remain at rest or in motion unless some external force is applied to it.*

The skater uses his leg muscles to exert pressure through the blade against the ice. The blade is used in a thrusting motion to the side while force is applied downward through the other leg in a forward direction. The blade directed forward will continue, gradually slowing because of friction between ice and blade. To stop quickly, the blades may be turned at right angles to the direction of movement, causing maximum friction against the ice.

Newton's Second Law of Motion—*The rate at which the momentum of a body changes is equal to the force acting and takes place in the direction of a straight line through which the resultant force acts.*

For skaters this means that the more the body weight can be put into the push, the faster they will go. The opposite is true for stopping. The more they use body weight to help, the quicker they will stop. So, the faster the skating, the greater the force required to stop.

Newton's Third Law of Motion—*For every force which acts on a body, there is an equal and opposite reaction which acts on some other body.*

When a skater pushes his blade against the edge of the ice, the ice pushes back. Skaters move along the ice because their mass is small compared to that of the ice which will not move.

Can you apply these laws to baseball and/or basketball?

1. Why does the ball bounce higher when thrown against the floor than when dropped?

   _____

   _____

2. Spin the ball on the floor like a top. How long does it continue? What is necessary to make it stop? _____

   _____

3. When you catch a thrown ball, how does your body absorb the energy from the ball?

   _____

   _____

4. How do the laws explain the action of a batter striking a ball?

   _____

   _____

5. What laws affect the motion of a fielder chasing a baseball or a basketball player making a rebound? Explain _____

   _____

   _____

Sonja Henie
(1912–1969)

Sonja Henie was born in Oslo, Norway, on April 8, 1912. Her father had been a bicycle racing champion. Sonja took ballet lessons from five years of age, and was given a pair of skates on the Christmas following her sixth birthday. Her older brother was her first teacher. She proved to be a talented student and by age 10 had won the Norwegian ladies title. When she was 11, she competed in the Olympics, finishing last in her group. Her father increased his support, hiring the best teachers available, including the great Russian ballerina Tamara Karsavina.

Sonja Henie made skating exciting by combining ballet movements with athletic jumps and spins. Her skating told a story with higher jumps and faster spins than anyone before her. Her programs were graceful, well practiced, and confident. Sonja Henie became the first woman to wear silk tights and short skirts. She was a skater as well as an artist, and the public loved her. She first performed in the United States in 1930.

During her career, Sonja Henie won six European titles (1931–1936), 10 world championships (1927–1936), and three Olympic gold medals (1928, 1932, 1936). No woman skater has ever won more or had such a profound effect on her sport. In 1936, she became a professional skater, working with promoter Arthur Wirtz. She starred in several American movies for Twentieth Century-Fox, once ranking third behind Siirley Temple and Clark Gable as a box office attraction and earning more than 200,000 dollars a year—a fortune at the time. She formed the first Hollywood Ice Revues, consistent money makers. In time she progressed from star to owner, becoming a multi-millionaire in her own right. In 1956, Sonja married millionaire Nils Onstad and had homes in Norway and Bel Air, California. The couple donated an art museum and cultural center to the city of Oslo. Sonja Henie died of leukemia on October 12, 1969. She was 57 years old.

Suggested Activities and Extensions

1. Locate Norway on a map of the world. Read more about the country, particularly its geography and climate. Why is skating a popular sport there? What other sports are important in the Scandinavian countries?

2. One of Sonja Henie's contributions to figure skating was the change in costume from ankle–length dark dresses, wide brim hats, and black boots to silk stockings and skirts worn above the knee. Look at pictures of several modern figure–skaters. How are their costumes designed to enhance the performance? Would they be able to skate in ankle-length dresses? Choose theme music appropriate for a skating program and design a costume to fit the event.

3. Discuss the influence of Sonja's ballet training on her skating. Watch figure-skating videos and point out the balletic moves of the skaters. How does dance enhance the performance?

4. Sonja Henie became a United States citizen while she was touring the country in the Hollywood Ice Revues. Research what an immigrant must do to be granted citizenship.

   - How old must one be?
   - What must be learned?
   - Must a test be taken?
   - How long does the process take?

5. Sonja Henie won her first world title at age 13. How do you think that kind of fame affects a 13-year old? What would it mean to you? If you had been her parents, what kind of advice would you have given Sonja?

6. What advances in technology and training have taken place since Sonja Henie's time to help skaters improve their performances?

   - Skate design:
   - Rink maintenance:
   - Physical (muscle) training:
   - Dietary knowledge:
   - Coaching:

7. Some figure-skating movements of today are completely new or have been dropped (the figure eight, for example) from international competition. See if you can find out what moves are common today that were not done in Sonja Henie's day and what moves are still performed (the axel, for instance). Construct a Venn diagram to illustrate these changes.

Related Reading _____

From Axels to Zambonis by Dan Gutman. Penguin, 1995.
Great Skates by Laura Hilgers. Little, Brown, 1991.
Ice Skating by Tom Wood. Watts, 1990.
Norway by Ralph Zickgraf. Chelsea, 1989.
The Olympic Games by Theodore Knight. Lucent, 1991.
Skating by Donna Bailey. Raintree, 1990.
The Young Dancer by Darcey Bussell. Dorling Kindersley, 1994.

A Lifetime of Accomplishment

On her induction into the Figure Skating Hall of Fame, Sonja Henie was recognized as holding the women's record for the most world championships (10) and Olympic gold medals (3). She was also the European women's champion six times.

Use this page to design a display in her honor.

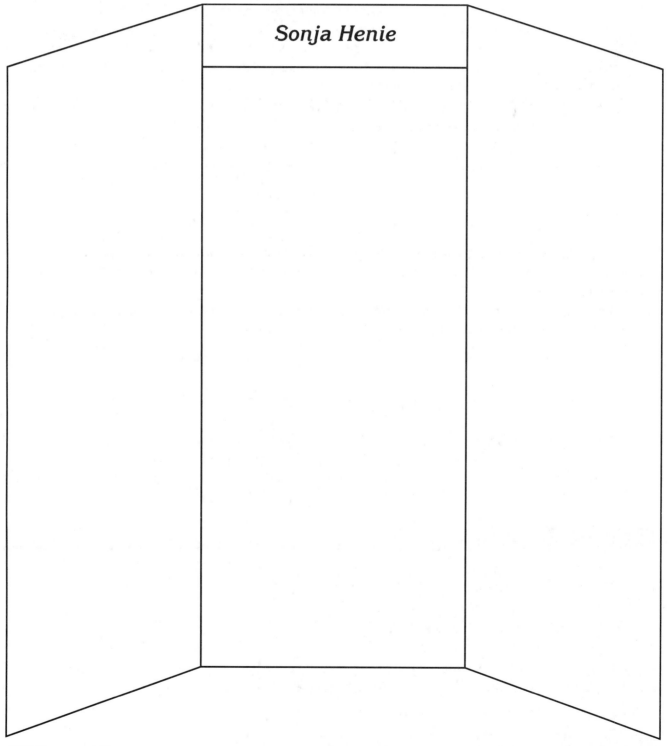

Sonja Henie

Torvill and Dean

(1957–) (1958–)

Jayne Torvill and Christopher Dean were both born in Nottingham, England. They are from middle class backgrounds—Jayne's parents owned a news agents' shop, and Chris's father was an electrician. Jayne began skating at age nine, and Chris took up the sport after receiving skates for Christmas when he was 10 years old.

In 1971 Jayne Torvill won the British senior pairs championship with her partner, Michael Hutchinson. The next year Hutchinson moved to London, and Torvill continued in solo skating competition. Christopher Dean began as an ice dancer with partner Sandra Elson. They were the British junior dance champions in 1974.

In 1975 Janet Sawbridge, a professional skater and mutual friend, suggested that Jayne and Chris try skating together. The pair enjoyed working together and made excellent progress. Janet was their coach and trainer.

By 1976 they were ready for European competitions in St. Gervais, France, and Obserstdorf, Germany. The pair entered the European and world championships in the winter of 1978. They began work with a new coach, Betty Callaway, following the world championships in Ottawa, Canada. She encouraged Torvill and Dean to polish their program, and in 1978 they became the British ice skating champions. They continued to improve their standing in international tournaments. In 1980 Jayne Torvill and Chris Dean decided to leave their jobs to devote themselves to skating full time.

As a reward for commitment to their sport, Torvill and Dean placed first in all 1981 competitions, making them the British, European, and world champions in ice dancing. The pair began to develop their own choreography around a central theme for both short programs and free dance competitions. In 1984 their skating ability and creative choreography reached a high point with the free dance to Maurice Ravel's *Bolero*. They performed the dramatic love story at the 1984 Olympics in Sarajevo and became the only team in figure skating history to receive perfect 6.0 scores from all judges. Torvill and Dean returned to the Olympics 10 years later (1994) and won a bronze medal.

Jayne Torvill and Christopher Dean turned professional after the 1984 Olympics and toured the world with Ice Capades. Free from the restrictive rules of competitions, they have been able to bring their most innovative interpretations to ice dancing.

Suggested Activities and Extensions

1. Locate Nottingham, England; St. Gervais, France; Obserstdorf, Germany; Ottawa, Canada; Lake Placid, New York; Sarajevo, Yugoslavia; and Lillehammer, Norway, on a map of the world.

2. Compare/contrast skating with a partner and solo skating. What must a pair consider to be successful in competition? Is good technical skating enough to become champions? Discuss.

3. Listen to Maurice Ravel's *Bolero*. This was the music that Torvill and Dean used for their free dance in the Winter Olympics (1984) that won perfect scores for artistic impression. Why is this piece a good choice for skating/dancing music?

4. Torvill and Dean are the only team to have been awarded nine perfect 6.0 scores from all judges in world competitions. Discuss the importance of this achievement, considering the subjectivity of judging. Is it easy to get a perfect score on a math test? On a writing assignment?

5. Do research to learn the names and countries of five other ice dancing pairs. List any awards or honors if applicable.

6. In what ways is ice dancing more difficult (or easier) than ballet? Are jumps and spins more difficult on ice or easier? Why? Interview both a dancer and a skater to see if you can get some clear answers to these questions.

7. Ballet dancers and ice dancers are both athletes. Is the training of one type of athlete more demanding than that of the other? Can you find out the average amount of time spent in practice and daily training for professionals (or top amateurs) in each endeavor?

8. Research the types of sports injuries most common among skaters. Make a list of those injuries, the best treatment for each, and the best training routines to guard against them.

9. Pair skating and ice dancing are two separate events in amateur and professional competition. Research the differences between the two and, using stick figures, illustrate two moves performed in pair skating that are not allowed in ice dancing. Add a written explanation to the illustrations.

10. Create a labeled stick-figure diagram of these three classic ice dancing positions:
    - the hand-in-hand position
    - the Kilian position
    - the closed position

    Combine these illustrations with those described in activity nine to create a display on ice dancing and pair dancing.

Related Reading

Great Skates by Laura Hilgers. Little, Brown, 1991.
Ice Dancing Illustrated by Lorna Dyer. Moore Publications, 1980.
Ice Skating by Tom Wood. Watts, 1990.
The Olympic Games by Theodore Knight. Lucent, 1991.
Skating by Donna Bailey. Raintree, 1990.
Torvill and Dean: Ice Dancing's Perfect Pair by Frann Shuker-Haines. Blackbirch Marketing, Inc., 1995.

Dance Partners Venn Diagram

Compare and contrast Jayne Torvill and Christopher Dean on a Venn Diagram. Remember to use this information from your reading:

- age each began skating
- where they were born
- first skating partners

- coaches and trainers
- competitions
- Ice Capades

- *Bolero*
- perfect Olympics scores

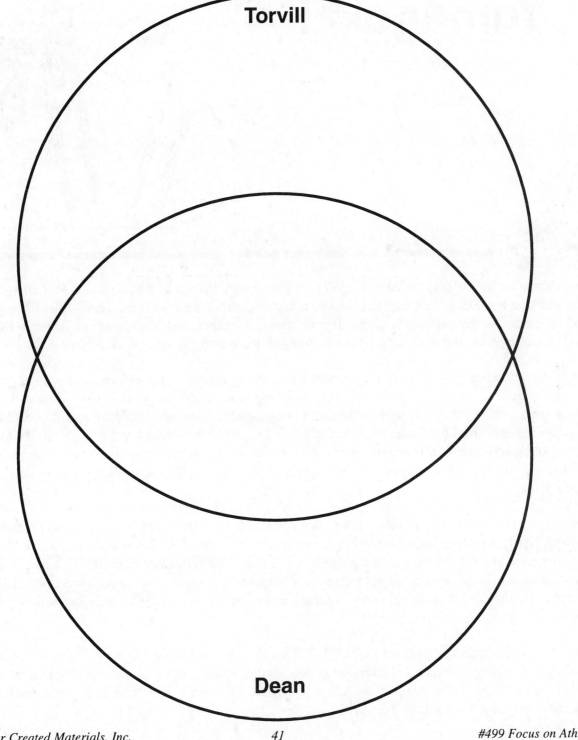

Torvill

Dean

Kristi Yamaguchi
(1971–)

Kristi Yamaguchi was born on July 12, 1971, in Fremont, California. She had club feet and needed to wear casts on her feet for a year. Kristi wore corrective shoes for four more years. She has a younger brother, Brett, and an older sister, Lori. Her mother is a medical secretary, and her father is a dentist. Kristi became interested in skating after watching an ice skating show at a local mall.

While still attending school every day, Kristi began taking lessons. She entered and won her first contest at age six. At age seven, Kristi began working with singles coach, Christy Kjarsgaard. Four days a week, Kristi would get up at 4:00 a.m. to begin her lessons at a shopping mall in San Mateo, about 30 minutes from her home. She would skate for five hours while her mother waited. At 10:00 they would go to school in Fremont. After school, she would hurry to another rink and work with pairs coach Jim Hulick and Kristi's partner, Rudi Galindo. By age 10, this schedule was increased to six days a week.

She worked very hard and, because of her talent, was able to compete in both pairs and singles events. In 1989, Kristi and Rudi had advanced to the senior level in the U.S. Nationals and won the gold medal. She continued skating doubles until the death of her pairs coach in December 1989. Kristi won the silver medal for her singles performance in that competition. After high school graduation, Kristi moved to Canada to live with her newly married coach. Kristi missed her family but believed the move was necessary to further her career.

In the World Championships prior to the 1992 Olympics, Kristi finished first, followed by Tonya Harding and Nancy Kerrigan. She arrived at Albertville, France, ready to win, having perfected the triple axel. Almost all the competitors fell except Kristi. She was clearly the first-place winner—the greatest female figure skater in the world.

Suggested Activities and Extensions

1. How would Kristi's life have been different without the encouragement of her parents? They were willing to sacrifice to pay for Kristi's training. What adults are important to your development? How do they influence your accomplishments?

2. What would be the advantages and/or disadvantages of being the brother or sister of an award-winning athlete?

3. Kristi improved her skating by studying videotapes of her performances. Help your students improve by taping them giving speeches, book reports, or musical performances. Discuss why watching yourself do something is very informative.

4. Training a skater can be very expensive. Visit a sporting goods store to learn the prices of skates. Contact rinks for the cost of lessons and practice time and interview costumers for the price of costumes. Make a chart of the expenses and estimate the total cost for a year of training. Don't forget the cost of transportation to and from the lessons.

5. Listen to some of the music from Puccini's *Madame Butterfly* that Kristi used for her Olympic short program. Discuss its significance to her Japanese American heritage.

6. Read more about Dorothy Hamill, another gold medal skater and Kristi's idol.

7. Many people go to outdoor and indoor skating rinks for recreation purposes—not to watch others but to skate themselves, even though they may not be superior athletes. What do you suppose professional skaters do for recreation? What other sports might attract them? Is it possible that certain sports might not be good for them to practice because they might interfere with skating proficiency? (Some professional athletes are forbidden by their contracts to engage in some other sports activities because of the chances of injury.) Make a list of professional skaters and have the members of your class write letters surveying the skaters' favorite recreational activities. Chart the results.

8. Safety is an important element in any sport. Protective pads, helmets, and gloves are now commonplace for rollerblading activities, for example. What are the standard precautions that should be taken for ice skating? Interview an ice skating teacher, coach, or other experienced skater to develop a list of safety rules on the ice. Design a poster for classroom or local ice rink display.

9. Great success in athletics sometimes leads to opportunities in other commercial fields, especially advertising. Kristi Yamaguchi has served as a spokesperson for several commercial enterprises. Find out what products and/or services she has endorsed. Contact a local advertising agency for information on what such top stars are sometimes paid for their endorsements. (The golfer Tiger Woods was reportedly paid 40 million dollars to endorse Nike products—certainly an unusually high fee.)

Related Reading

Figure Skating by Margaret Ryan. Watts, 1987.
Ice Skating by Tom Wood. Watts, 1990.
Kristi Yamaguchi: Artist on Ice by Shiobhan Donahue. Lerner Group, 1993.
Kristi Yamaguchi: Pure Gold by Jeff Savage. Dillon, 1993.

Olympic Figure Skating Scoring

There are nine judges in Olympic figure skating competitions. Each one rates the skating performance from 0–6, using decimal points for exact placements. Then the scores from each judge are compared. The skater receiving the highest mark from a particular judge is placed first by that judge. The skater with the most first place rankings is the winner.

Look at these scores and determine which skaters received the gold, silver, and bronze medals. (These were actual scores for technical merit.)

Judges	1	2	3	4	5	6	7	8	9
Kristi	5.7	5.7	5.7	5.7	5.7	5.8	5.8	5.8	5.8
Mary	5.5	5.8	5.6	5.6	5.5	5.7	5.6	5.6	5.5
Jane	5.6	5.6	5.8	5.5	5.8	5.6	5.7	5.7	5.6

Now organize the skaters into 1st, 2nd, and 3rd place for each judge.

Judges	1	2	3	4	5	6	7	8	9
1st									
2nd									
3rd									

Now decide the medal winners by determining which skaters have the most 1st, 2nd, and 3rd place scores.

Gold _____ Silver _____ Bronze _____

Fold under.

Answers:

Judges	1	2	3	4	5	6	7	8	9
1st	Kristi	Mary	Jane	Kristi	Jane	Kristi	Kristi	Kristi	Kristi
2nd	Jane	Kristi	Kristi	Mary	Kristi	Mary	Jane	Jane	Jane
3rd	Mary	Jane	Mary	Jane	Mary	Jane	Mary	Mary	Mary

Gold: *Kristi*   Silver: *Jane*   Bronze: *Mary*

Football

The first organized game of football was played between Princeton University and Rutgers University in New Jersey on November 6, 1869. There were 25–30 players on each team. The object was to kick a ball over the opponent's goal line. Until the early 1900s, football was mainly a college sport.

Walter Camp, the "Father of American Football," created these rules for the game about 1880. There were 11 players per side, a system of downs, yards gained, and a center snap. The field was marked with yard lines. There was no protective equipment, and players were frequently injured. In 1906, the forward pass was introduced as a means of spreading the players over the field.

The object of the game is to score a touchdown by running or passing the ball over the opponent's goal line. College and professional games are divided into two halves, each 30 minutes long. The teams change direction after each quarter. A football field is 100 yards long, marked with solid white lines every five yards. There is a goal post at each end of the field on the back line of the end zone. There are four ways to score in football: the touchdown (6), point after touchdown (1), field goal (3), and a safety (2). Each professional and college team is made up of separate defensive and offensive teams.

The offensive team includes the offensive linemen, backfield, and receivers. The linemen are usually the biggest players on the team. Their main job is to block on running and passing plays. The quarterback and running backs are part of the backfield. The quarterback calls the plays and can throw or pass the ball to a running back. Running backs must be strong and able to run very fast. The receivers are fast runners who catch passes thrown by the quarterback. The offense has four plays (downs) in which to move the ball at least 10 yards.

The defensive team includes the defensive linemen, linebackers, and secondary. There are usually four linemen—two tackles and two ends. When the quarterback is passing, the defensive linemen try to tackle (sack) him. When there is a running play, the defensive linemen try to tackle the ball carrier. There are usually three linebackers who defend against the run and pass play. They must be very strong and able to run fast. The secondary is made up of four defensive backs. Their job is to cover pass receivers if they manage to slip past the linemen and linebackers. It is the job of the defense to stop the offense from gaining a first down.

Professional football was first sponsored by athletic clubs in large cities. In 1920 13 teams formed the American Professional Football Association. Jim Thorpe was named president. Two years later, it became the National Football League.

For more information write to the following addresses:

- National Football League
  410 Park Avenue
  New York, New York 10022

- Pro Football Hall of Fame
  21211 George Halas Dr. N.W.
  Canton, Ohio 44708

Joe Montana

(1956–)

An only child, Joseph C. Montana was born June 11, 1956, in Monongahela, Pennsylvania, near Pittsburgh. Joe Montana, senior, had been an excellent athlete in the navy and hoped that his son would share his interest in sports. After all, Western Pennsylvania had been the source of several other famous quarterbacks—Johnny Unitas, Dan Marino, Terry Hanratty, and Joe Namath.

Father and son spent time together shooting baskets, hitting baseballs, and passing a football through a tire swing that hung in a neighbor's yard. Young Joe developed into a well-rounded athlete who competed in high school baseball, basketball, and football. Upon graduation, he turned down a basketball scholarship to North Carolina State and went to Notre Dame to play football under coach Dan Devine. At Notre Dame he became known as "The Comeback Kid" because he was able to lead his team to victory during the final minutes of a game.

He was drafted by coach Bill Walsh to play professional football for the San Francisco 49ers in 1979. He became the starting quarterback in 1981 and on January 24, 1982, led the team to victory in Super Bowl XVI against the Cincinnati Bengals. He was the Most Valuable Player (MVP) of that game. After the 1983 season, Joe married Jennifer Wallace, a model and television actress. They have three children.

In 1986 Joe suffered a ruptured disk which might have ended his playing career, but he underwent surgery, followed a difficult rehabilitation program, and was back on the field just 55 days after the injury. The 49ers won the 1988 Super Bowl, even though Joe was having trouble with a swollen right elbow for most of the season.

Montana had the best season in history for any NFL quarterback in 1989 . He was named NFL Player of the Year by the Associated Press, and Offensive Player of the Year by both Associated Press and United Press International. He was honored as Sportsman of the Year by *Sporting News* and Player of the Year by *Sports Illustrated*. Joe was named to the NFL All-Pro and All-Star teams. He had the highest pass efficiency rating in NFL history in 1989, leading the team to another Super Bowl championship. Other records included the most pass completions in a post-season game and the most passing yards in a Super Bowl. After that season, he needed surgery on his left knee. It was his fifth operation since 1983, and his second operation on the same knee.

In 1991, Joe was forced to miss the season because of surgery for a torn tendon in his right elbow. Steve Young, his replacement, was the NFL's Most Valuable Player for 1992. It became clear that Joe would no longer be the starting quarterback for the 49ers. He asked to be traded. In April 1993 Joe was traded to the Kansas City Chiefs to be their starting quarterback. Joe Montana retired from football on April 19, 1995. Celebrations in his honor were held in Kansas City and San Francisco.

Suggested Activities and Extensions

1. Brainstorm a list of other star quarterbacks in NFL history. Learn more information about at least one other former quarterback from Western Pennsylvania.

2. Make a list of important character traits for a quarterback— for example, confidence, intelligence, leadership, etc. How are those characteristics beneficial in everyday life?

3. How might Joe Montana's career have been different if he had chosen to attend North Carolina State on a basketball scholarship? Why do you think he made a wise decision in choosing football?

4. Joe Montana was plagued by injuries for much of his career. Invite a sports medicine doctor or therapist to talk to your class about rehabilitation after sports injuries. Discuss ways that student athletes may protect themselves from injuries.

5. Research the most common sports injuries in football. Determine which injuries are potentially most dangerous or considered to be career ending. Why is the quarterback considered the position most vulnerable to injury? What is arthroscopic surgery?

6. What is the average size and weight of a professional quarterback? How does this compare to the average size and weight of professional linemen? Locate some actual figures for these positions among players on the field today. Compare their sizes to members of your class and make some scale models cut from construction paper to illustrate the differences.

7. If possible, ask your physical education teacher to give students an opportunity to try throwing a football through a suspended tire. That's the way Joe practiced with his father!

8. Learn the special rules in the NFL concerning legal and illegal (or penalty-causing) sacks of the quarterback. What is the purpose of having these special rules for the quarterback? Discuss.

9. Some colleges and universities have become well known for their emphasis on football, producing large numbers of players who go on to become professional players and stars. Joe Montana attended Notre Dame University. Find out where Notre Dame is and write their publicity and/or athletic department for information on other professional players who attended the school. Prepare an alphabetical list of Notre Dame alumni who became successful professional players.

10. For more information about Joe Montana or current players, write to the following address:

    San Francisco 49ers
    4949 Centennial Blvd.
    Santa Clara, California 95054

Related Reading

Dan Fouts, Ken Anderson, Joe Theismann and Other All-Time Great Quarterbacks by Phyllis and Zander Hollander. Random House, 1983.

Joe Montana by Bob Italia. Abdo & Daughters, 1992.

Joe Montana by Marc Appleman. Little, Brown, 1991.

Joe Montana: Comeback Quarterback by Thomas R. Raber. Lerner Group, 1990.

The San Francisco 49ers by Steve Potts. Creative Education, 1991.

San Francisco 49ers: The Super Years by Glenn Dickey. Chronicle, 1989.

Montana Injured!

Joe suffered a painful spinal injury during the 49ers 1986 season opener against Tampa Bay. When he returned to San Francisco, tests showed that he had a ruptured disk in his lower back. The news was bad. Joe needed surgery, and doctors said he might never play football again.

How do you think Joe took this news?

On September 15, 1986, all the major newspapers in San Francisco carried the story of Joe's operation.

- It took doctors two and a half hours to remove the damaged disk.
- His parents and teammates Dwight Clark, Ronnie Lott, and Wendell Tyler visited the hospital.
- There was a special telephone hotline hooked up to give fans information about Joe's condition.
- Joe was determined to return to football.
- He walked around his room for 10 minutes the day after surgery.
- Three days after the operation, he was exercising.
- On the fourth day he began lifting weights.
- The seventh day following surgery, Joe walked a mile to and from rehabilitation. He was released from the hospital.

Use these facts to recreate one of the articles that might have appeared in a San Francisco newspaper about Joe's injury.

Jerry Rice

(1962–)

Jerry Lee Rice was born in Starkville, Mississippi, on October 13, 1962. He has two sisters and five brothers. The family lived in a small town of 500 people without sidewalks or traffic lights. Jerry enjoyed playing football and basketball as a child. He believes that working with his father (a bricklayer) helped him gain the strength and hand-to-eye coordination that made him a great receiver. In addition, running five miles to high school each day and chasing the neighbor's horses helped Jerry become a powerful runner.

In high school, Jerry averaged 30 points a game in basketball and was on the track team. He did not consider playing football until it was suggested to him by the vice principal who caught him skipping class. Jerry ran from him so quickly that the vice principal said the football team could use a player with his speed. He was given a choice to try out for football or serve a detention. That was a punishment that changed his life.

Because he lived in such a small town, Jerry's excellent play went unnoticed by major college recruiters, unfortunately. He accepted a scholarship offer from Coach Archie Cooley to attend Mississippi Valley State University. He studied auto mechanics and physical education. Jerry set 18 Division I-AA records, including most catches, touchdowns, and receiving yards. He was an All-American. His natural ability and outstanding performances got the attention of NFL coaches. Jerry was drafted by the San Francisco 49ers after college graduation in April 1985.

In the beginning, Jerry had a difficult time adjusting to pro football and the big city fans. In the first eight games, he dropped 10 passes and made many mistakes. He was becoming very frustrated when Joe Montana took an interest in him. They spent time together practicing and talking about football. Joe believed in him, and soon the pair became so friendly they could almost read each other's minds on the field. Jerry Rice became Joe's favorite receiver.

In 1991 Jerry became the youngest player to catch 500 passes in a career. He is the 49ers' all-time leader in receptions, receiving yards, and touchdowns. He has played in seven Pro Bowls, 1987–1993. Players and coaches admire his natural athletic ability, inner drive, and commitment to the game. Jerry's goal has always been to be the best receiver in the NFL.

Suggested Activities and Extensions

1. What do you think Jerry Rice would like to say today to the vice principal who required him to try out for football as punishment for skipping class? Write a dialogue that might take place between them as they meet by chance on a San Francisco street.

2. Jerry's performance on the field improved tremendously after he studied and learned the 49ers' playbook. Apply this experience to your life. Are there ever any shortcuts to success? How important is it to be willing to work hard in order to do well? Ask your high school coach to share his team's playbook. Look at the diagrams and discuss the problem of memorizing so many plays.

3. Ask your physical education teacher to set up an obstacle course for running practice. Try having someone pass the runners a football to simulate the job of a receiver.

4. For more information about Jerry Rice or current players, write to the following address:

   San Francisco 49ers
   4949 Centennial Blvd.
   Santa Clara, California 95054

5. Jerry's willingness to work hard has been the key to his success. He says, "If you want to be the best, you have to work at it." What do you want to be? How will you work to achieve your goals? Outline a plan for your life five and 10 years into the future. Which do you think is more important—natural talent or a strong work ethic? Explain.

6. Can a good receiver make a passer look better than he really is? How?

7. Can a good passer make a receiver look better than he really is? How?

8. Write a sports page article explaining how the teamwork between a passer and receiver is somehow more tightly needed than it is between a receiver and a blocking back.

9. What are the special rules that protect a receiver when he is running down the field to catch a pass? Why do you suppose those rules were passed?

10. Explain how a receiver can be guilty of offensive pass interference. (Check with a coach or library to research the rules of football.)

11. Design and create a board game that features Jerry Rice catching passes to advance to a touchdown. Remember to include penalties, interceptions, tackles, and out-of-bounds catches, along with the spectacular successes Rice was known for. The background of the board design, of course, might well be a replica of a football gridiron. Cards, spinners, or dice might be used to determine advances and/or retreats as the downs proceed.

Related Reading

Jerry Rice by Glenn Dickey. Enslow, 1993.

Jerry Rice by John Rolfe. Bantam, 1993.

Jerry Rice: Touchdown Talent by Edward Evans. Lerner, 1993.

The San Francisco 49ers by Steve Potts. Creative Education, 1991.

San Francisco 49ers: The Super Years by Glenn Dickey. Chronicle, 1989.

Jim Thorpe

(1888–1953)

James Francis Thorpe was born May 28, 1888, in Indian territory near Prague, Oklahoma. His father was half Irish and half Indian, and his mother was the granddaughter of the Chippewa chief Black Hawk. He was given the Indian name "Bright Path." Jim grew up in the one-room house where he was born. In 1904 he was sent to the Carlisle Indian School in Pennsylvania to be trained as a tailor. Jim played on the school's football and track teams, achieving great success.

He competed in the 1912 Olympics in Stockholm, Sweden, and won gold medals in the decathlon and pentathlon. Unfortunately, he was later asked to return his medals when it was discovered that he had played baseball for $25 a week. In those days, Olympic athletes were all unpaid amateurs. His heirs were presented with duplicate medals in 1982 after years of fighting to have his name restored to the Olympic record books. Jim had gone on to beat his own Olympic records in the hurdles, high jumps, pole vaults, and distance runs. It is said that Jim was a winner in every sport he tried, including tennis, billiards, wrestling, archery, lacrosse, basketball, hockey, swimming, bowling, and golf.

He returned to Carlisle to play football. He seemed unbeatable, setting up plays and scoring 29 touchdowns during the 1912 season. Jim became a professional baseball player when he signed a $5,000 contract with the New York Giants. Playing outfield, his lifetime batting average in major league baseball was .252. He later played with the Boston Braves and the Cincinnati Reds.

From 1915–1923, he returned to football and played for the Canton Bulldogs. Jim Thorpe organized his own football team, the Oorang Indians, in 1923, but no official records were kept. He retired at 41 after playing 15 years of professional ball but returned the following summer to minor league baseball.

After his career as America's greatest all-round male athlete, Jim fell into hard times during the Depression, often working at menial jobs for low wages. He died of a heart attack on March 28, 1953. Sportswriter Grantland Rice remembered Thorpe this way: "He could do more things well, even up to the point of brilliance, than any other player in the game."

Suggested Activities and Extensions

1. Historians say that Jim Thorpe ran the 100-yard dash in 10 seconds flat. Set up a 100-yard path on the playground and record your students' best times. On another day, measure how many yards your students can run in 10 seconds.

2. In field events, Jim once high-jumped six feet five inches and long-jumped 24 feet. Measure these distances and give your students the opportunity to compete in these events.

3. One characteristic of some cultures is that they tend to play for the good of the team rather than personal glory. Discuss how this applies to our culture and why it might or might not be an especially desirable trait among athletes. Is it possible for such a characteristic to be good in one situation (or sport) and not so good in another? Discuss.

4. Jim Thorpe was the Joe Montana or Deion Sanders of his day. How would his life and career have been different if he had made a huge salary and had the advantage of modern publicity?

5. Early football had its beginnings in the rules of rugby and soccer. Read more about those sports to determine the similarities and differences with modern American football.

6. Research the type of schooling provided to Native Americans living on reservations in this country. Has it been segregated? Has it been beneficial to all? Is it different now from the way it was in Thorpe's day? Why were boarding schools such a common practice? Did the athletic experiences of Native American culture differ from those of the rest of the country? If so, in what ways?

7. The history of many athletes contains elements of hardship—overcoming physical, economic, social, family, or personal difficulties. If this is true of Jim Thorpe, how did his struggle differ from or appear similar to the struggles of other great athletes? In what ways do the struggles of a great athlete relate to the lives of ordinary persons?

8. Using stick figures, prepare drawings illustrating the method of high jumping in Jim Thorpe's day and the method used throughout the world today. Write an explanation for the changes in methods and techniques.

9. Prepare an illustrated report on the differences between the football helmet worn by Jim Thorpe and the helmet that is worn by today's players. Extend this report to show an illustrated development of other protective headgear, from military helmets to contemporary construction hard hats. Include other sports such as boxing, wrestling, bicycling, rollerblading, etc. Drawings, magazine cutouts, time lines, and collages are all possibilities for this activity.

Related Reading

The Chippewa by Alice Osinski. Children's Press, 1987.

Jim Thorpe by Carl R. Green and William R. Sanford. Silver Burdett, 1992.

Jim Thorpe: Legendary Athlete by Barbara Long. Enslow Publications, 1997.

Jim Thorpe: Twentieth Century Jock by Robert Lipsyte. HarperCollins, 1993.

The Olympic Summer Games by Carolina Arnold. Watts, 1991.

Early Football

Football was a young sport during Jim Thorpe's lifetime. The game was played with different rules by every team, and it was always violent. Harvard University players invented the "flying wedge" formation where linemen held onto each other by suitcase handles sewn to the backs of their uniforms. The ball carrier was protected while running down the field inside the "wedge." The flying wedge was made illegal in 1906 because of injuries.

The T-formation was invented in 1890 by Amos Alonzo Stagg, a player at Yale University. The center and quarterback form the trunk of the T, and the backs line up behind them parallel to the line of scrimmage. The T has become the standard football formation. Stagg invented several formations to make the game safer while coaching at the University of Chicago.

Although early rules kept changing, the influence of Harvard on the rules of football was strong until 1894, when the Intercollegiate Football Association was dissolved. The first professional football game in the United States was played the year following, 1895. In that year a rules committee dominated by the Yale graduate and football pioneer Walter Camp was formed by the influential eastern schools. In 1905 an independent group of colleges also formed a rules committee which soon merged with Camp's group to become the parent group presently governing American collegiate football.

In that same year, 1905, 18 people died and 159 were seriously injured playing football. President Theodore Roosevelt threatened to ban the game until it was made safer. The forward pass was legalized in 1906 but was not commonly used until the mid-1930s. Even after passing became accurate, running backs were the biggest attraction in the young NFL. Jim Thorpe excited fans with his strong running style.

In 1920 the American Professional Football Association (which became the National Football League one year later) organized with 22 teams. Jim Thorpe was elected president of the association.

Assignments

- Discuss and/or write: Do you think that modern football is too violent?

- What could Jim Thorpe contribute to the new football association?

- Make diagrams of a football field with the players lined up in the flying wedge and T-formations.

- Research early equipment and uniforms. Find pictures of early players. How does modern equipment protect players?

- Watch a football game on television. Make notes and report to the class about the play of running backs and quarterbacks.

- Design three offensive football plays. (Interview a coach or physical education teacher for advice.) Use X's to represent offensive players and O's to represent defensive players. Assemble all the plays from each student into a class playbook. Divide the class into teams for a game of touch football and, using the plays in the playbook, test which ones are the most successful.

Herschel Walker

(1962–)

Herschel Junior Walker was born on March 3, 1962, in Augusta, Georgia. He lived with his six brothers and sisters in the small town of Wrightsville, Georgia. His father worked in a clay processing factory, and his mother worked in a clothing factory. Herschel was well behaved and a good student. He enjoyed playing sports with his brothers and sisters, particularly his sister Veronica, who was an excellent runner. At age 12, Herschel began to do push-ups, sit-ups, and sprints to build strength and speed.

Herschel became one of the country's best high school football players with a record 6,137 yards rushing and 86 touchdowns. He was also a track star. He graduated from Johnson County High School with a 93 average. Herschel Walker was always a good student. He had many scholarship offers.

Herschel chose to attend the University of Georgia and study criminology but left after three years to join the United States Football League (USFL). In 1982 as a junior, Herschel won the Heisman Trophy, awarded the nation's best college player. Herschel returned to college during the off season to finish his degree.

Herschel was the star player for the New Jersey Generals in the USFL, earning about 5.5 million dollars in three years. On March 31, 1983, Herschel married his girlfriend, Cindy. In 1985, he was named Most Valuable Player of the USFL, having scored 22 touchdowns. Unfortunately, things were not going well for the league. There was little interest from fans who were used to fall and winter football. In 1985 Herschel was signed as a free agent by the Dallas Cowboys.

Herschel worked hard to learn the Cowboys' system of football. In his first season with the Cowboys, he caught 76 passes, setting a new receiving and team record. He led the league in total yards, rushing (891 yards) and receiving (715 yards) in the 1987 season, and the National Football Conference (NFC) in 1988 with 1,514 yards rushing. In 1989 Herschel Walker was traded to the Minnesota Vikings.

His experience with the Vikings was disappointing. Herschel found that he had a difficult time with the Viking's style of offense. He joined the Philadelphia Eagles as a free agent on June 22, 1992, after being released by Minnesota. Two back-to-back 100-yard games got him off to a good start with his fourth professional team. He became the first Eagle to rush for 1,000 yards since 1985.

Suggested Activities and Extensions

1. Herschel Walker enjoyed reading and writing poetry. Try writing poetry using key words like FOOTBALL, COWBOYS, VIKINGS, or EAGLES in an acrostic.

   Examples:

Fun, fast—	**C**hampions	**E**very
Only the best	**O**vercome defeat, and	**A**thlete
Opponents can make	**W**inning means	**G**iving, striving, running
Touchdowns.	**B**elieving in yourself—	**L**ets the world see—
Believe in yourself	**O**nly	**E**ffort means
And trust	**Y**ou can	**S**uccess.
Luck and your	**S**trive for your own success.	
Love for the game.		

2. Look for more information about the USFL. How many teams were there? Who were some of the most famous players? How long did the league last? What problems caused its demise?

3. Herschel Walker completed his degree in criminal justice. Why do you think it was important to him to finish college? Do research to determine what careers are available to a person with this training.

4. Ask your physical education teacher to illustrate the correct way to do sit-ups and push-ups.

5. For more information about Herschel Walker or current players, write to the following:

   - The Dallas Cowboys
     1 Cowboy Parkway
     Irving, Texas 75063

   - Minnesota Vikings
     9520 Viking Drive
     Eden Prairie, Minnesota 55344

   - Philadelphia Eagles
     Veterans' Stadium
     Broad St. and Pattison Ave.
     Philadelphia, Pennsylvania 19148

Related Reading

The Dallas Cowboys by Brenda Calomera. Creative Education, 1991.
Football Rules in Pictures by Lud Duroska and Don Schiffer. Berkley Pub., 1991.
Herschel Walker by Jim Benagh. Enslow, 1990.
The Minnesota Vikings by Steve Potts. Creative Education, 1991.

Protective Equipment

A player can be seriously injured without the proper equipment.

In the 1900s players wore shin guards and leather helmets. Some players stuffed padding into oversized shirts and pants. Cleats were invented to help players run on mud and ice. Some players believed that equipment was for "sissies," but by 1960 all players were required to wear helmets, shoulder pads, pants, jerseys, and cleats. Today's players realize that equipment is important for avoiding injuries and protecting their million-dollar careers.

These are some of the most important pieces of equipment:

Helmet—This is the most important piece of equipment. It is made of a hard plastic-like substance. The best ones have inserts able to be pumped full of air to fit the player's head.

Face Mask—The mask is made of plastic bars that fit on the front of the helmet. There are several different styles, depending on the player's position. The quarterback often has only one horizontal bar, allowing maximum vision for passing but still providing some facial protection. The mask protects the face, nose, and mouth.

Shoulder Pads—Pads are made of hard plastic plates padded on the inside with air or foam. Players choose pads that will protect them comfortably without restricting their movements.

Thigh and Knee Pads—Thigh pads are made of hard plastic, coated with foam. Knee pads are thick, flexible foam. They are both designed to absorb the shock of the tackle.

Hip Pads—These pads are best worn inside a girdle-like garment under game pants. Players also use pads to protect their lower spine.

Shoes—Turf shoe soles are covered with tiny rubber studs that bite into the ground. (These, of course, are designed to be used on artificial turf (as opposed to real grass). Grass shoes have long rubber cleats that provide traction on grass or mud.

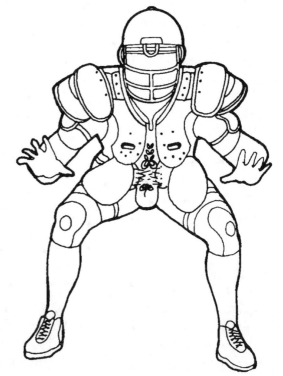

Every player realizes that football is a rough sport. All players must always be ready for physical contact. Being well equipped makes it possible to get through bumps and bruises and allows the player to concentrate on his job.

List equipment names below and draw arrows to the picture.

_____

_____

_____

_____

_____

Golf

Golf was first played in Scotland. In 1754, a group of golfers called the Society of St. Andrews set down rules for the sport. A golfer's score for the hole is equal to the number of strokes he needs to get from the tee to the cup. It usually takes 3, 4, or 5 shots to get into the hole, depending on the distance. *Par* is the average number of strokes a good player would need to move the ball from tee to cup. Golfers hope to score at or below par. A *birdie* is a score of one under par. An *eagle* is a score of two under par, and a hole-in-one (an *ace*) is when a golfer's first shot goes into the hole. A score of one above par is called a *bogey*. Two strokes over par is a *double bogey*, and three strokes over par is a *triple bogey*. The better the golfer, the lower his score will be.

Golf clubs and balls are the basic pieces of golf equipment. Balls have a dimpled plastic covering over a hard rubber center. They are usually white. Golf clubs have a head for hitting the ball and a grip which the golfer holds. The shaft, connecting the head and the grip, may be made of wood (rare today), steel, graphite, aluminum, or fiberglass. There are two types of golf clubs—woods and irons. The heads of modern "woods" are usually made of metal—steel or titanium, although some players still use the traditional wood. They are used to hit long, low, straight shots. Irons have smaller, thin heads made of steel. They are used for shorter, high-arching shots that must be very accurate. Players also use specialized clubs for specific shots like putts, chip shots, and playing out of heavy rough and bunkers. There are usually seven woods and 12 irons to choose from, but in competition a player may carry only 14 clubs in his or her bag.

The first golf courses were built in the United States in the 1880s. The United States Golf Association (USGA) for amateurs was formed in 1894. Championship golf began the next year at the Newport (Rhode Island) Country Club with the U.S. Open. One month later, the first women's amateur championship was held at the Meadow Brook Club in Hempstead, New York. The Professional Golfers Association of America (PGA) was formed in 1916. There are 50 events and over $55 million in prize money on the PGA Tour. Golfers over 50 years of age compete in the Senior PGA Tour.

The Women's Professional Golf Association (WPGA) was organized in 1944, and the first Women's Open was held in 1946. The WPGA was replaced by the Ladies Professional Golf Association (LPGA) in 1950. There are 38 tournaments and $21 million in prize money on the LPGA Tour.

For more information write to the following addresses:

- The United States Golf Association
  Golf House, P.O. Box 708
  Far Hills, New Jersey 07931-0708

- PGA World Golf Hall of Fame
  PGA Blvd.
  Pinehurst, NC 28374

- Professional Golfers Association
  Sawgrass
  112 TPC Blvd.
  Ponte Vedra, Florida 32082

Nancy Lopez

(1957–)

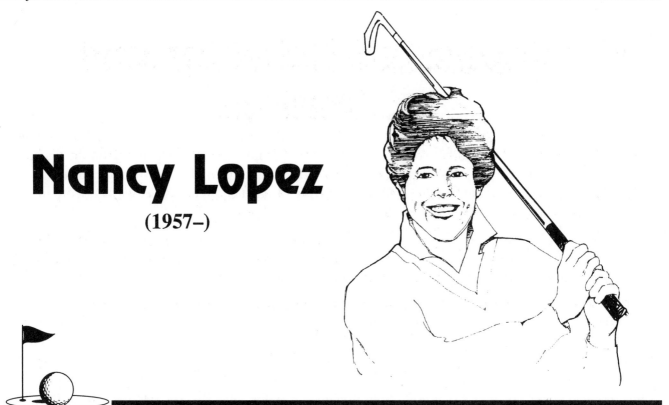

Nancy Lopez was born on January 6, 1957, in Torrance, California. She was raised in Roswell, New Mexico. Nancy became interested in golf as a child when her parents took up the game for her mother's health. Nancy won her first tournament at age nine. Her father was so proud that he gave her a Barbie doll, a tradition that has continued ever since. By age 11, she was a better golfer than either of her parents, and her father began to groom her for tournament play.

Nancy won the New Mexico Women's Amateur Championship when she was only 12. She was not permitted to play on the golf course at the local country club because she was a Mexican American, so it was difficult to improve her game. Nancy finished second in the Women's Open while still in high school and attended the University of Tulsa for two years on a golf scholarship. She studied engineering and business but chose to leave college to become a professional golfer.

She began her professional career in 1978 by winning nine tournaments, a record five in a row. At 22 Nancy married sportscaster Tim Melton, but the travel and pressures of being a professional athlete hurt her marriage. Nancy and Tim were divorced in 1982. She has been named Player of the Year four times, the first time as a rookie. Nancy has won three LPGA Championships, and with all these honors, the opportunity to endorse several golf products.

Lopez has ranked at the top of the pro circuit for her entire career. She had her best year in 1985, earning more money than any other player and winning five tournaments. At age 30, Nancy became the youngest golfer ever elected to the LPGA Hall of Fame. The LPGA Hall of Fame, incidentally, has been called the most difficult of all such athletic institutions to win a place in. It requires that the player win a minimum of 30 authorized tournaments to be considered for membership. No other professional sports association—men's or women's—has such a stringent requirement.

She is now married to Ray Knight of the Cincinnati Reds. The couple has three daughters—Ashley, Erinn, and Torri. She has cut back on tournament play to spend time with her family. She intends to continue playing golf as long as it is still fun for her.

Suggested Activities and Extensions

1. Work in groups to learn the names of at least five other famous Hispanic women. As a class, combine your lists and categorize by careers.

2. Learn more about Lee Trevino, a Mexican American professional golfer from Texas, a neighboring state of New Mexico where Nancy Lopez grew up.

3. Nancy's husband, Ray Knight, has been a manager/coach of the Cincinnati Reds. How do you think their marriage benefits from their involvement in pro sports? What would be some of the disadvantages of these high-stress, high-profile careers?

4. For more information about famous women golfers, write to the following source:

   Ladies Professional Golf Association
   2570 W. International Speedway Blvd., Suite B
   Daytona Beach, Florida 32114

5. If possible, arrange to hit practice balls in a field near your school. Measure the distances or learn to estimate them by stepping off the distances and converting them to yards.

6. After students have read Golf Grip, Stance, and Swing on page 60, reproduce the following exercise and have them number the items in proper sequence.

_____ A. It is important to learn the right way to grip a club.

_____ B. When you are ready to swing, turn sideways to the hole.

_____ C. Your body, hips, and shoulders are turned away from the hole at the top of your swing.

_____ D. The club rests in the palm of the left hand.

_____ E. Grip the club with your hands about six inches from your body.

_____ F. Your left shoulder moves under your chin as you begin your backswing.

_____ G. Be sure you stand with your back straight and your weight balanced on both feet.

_____ H. Keep your head level and keep your left arm straight.

_____ I. Hold the club between the first and second knuckles of the fingers of your right hand.

_____ J. Your body and hips turn towards the hole in the forward part of the swing.

Related Reading _____

Golf Basics by Roger Schiffman. Prentice-Hall, 1986.
The Junior Golf Book by Larry Hayes and Rhonda Glenn. St. Martin's Press, 1994.
Nancy Lopez by Craig Schumacher. Creative Education, 1979.
The Picture Story of Nancy Lopez by Betty Lou Phillips. Simon and Schuster, 1980.
Winning Women by Fred McMane and Catherine Wolf. Bantam, 1995.

Golf Grip, Stance, and Swing

Nancy Lopez began playing golf at the age of eight. She did not have any formal lessons. Here is some information about the golf swing that can help a junior player.

The first thing you must learn is the proper way to grip a club. The left hand should close firmly around the grip with the thumb lying on the top of the shaft. The club lies in the palm of the left hand. The grip is held between the first and second knuckles of the fingers of your right hand. The left thumb is covered by the crease of right palm. Your right thumb lies along the left side of the grip.

After you are able to grip the club correctly, you must learn the proper stance. With the ball in front of you, turn sideways to the hole. Grip the club with your arms about six inches away from your body. The back of your left hand should face the hole. Your back should be straight and your weight should be balanced.

As you begin your backswing, your left shoulder moves under your chin as your club moves away from the hole. Be sure to keep your head level and keep your left arm extended. At the top of the swing, your body, hips, and shoulders are turned away from the hole. In the forward swing, your body and hips turn towards the hole and your weight moves back to your left foot. It is important to maintain good balance throughout the swing. As you finish the swing, you should be facing the hole.

Fold under.

Answers:m (page 59, number 6)

A—1, B—5, C—9, D—2, E—4, F—7, G—6, H—8, I—3, J—10

Jack Nicklaus

(1940–)

Jack William Nicklaus was born January 21, 1940, in Columbus, Ohio. His father encouraged his son's interest in sports, giving him a set of clubs at age 10. He started taking lessons from a local golf pro and by age 16 had won the Ohio Open. In high school, Jack was also an excellent baseball and basketball player, but he always preferred golf.

While a business major at Ohio State University, Jack won two national amateur titles in 1959 and 1961. Playing with the American amateur team gave Jack the confidence he needed to finish second to Arnold Palmer in the 1960 U.S. Open. (Both professional and amateur players compete in open tournaments.) Jack became a professional golfer after that win.

In 1963 he became the youngest player ever to win the Masters with a two-under-par score of 286. He placed second in the Masters, PGA Championship, and British Open in 1964. In 1965 he shot a course record 271 (17 under par) to win the Masters at the Augusta National Golf Course in Georgia. Jack won the U.S. Open and was named PGA Player of the Year in 1967. He did not win another major tournament until 1970. (Two of Jack's records—the youngest Masters winner and the Masters low score—have since been eclipsed by Tiger Woods' performance in the 1997 Masters tournament.)

He returned to the tour with a trim physique and more fashionable clothes. He was nicknamed "The Golden Bear" because of his blond hair and fierce style of play. Jack won the 1970 British Open by a single stroke in the playoff round. The next year, he won the PGA Championship.

In 1972 Jack won the Masters and U.S. Open. He hoped to win the "Grand Slam" of golf by winning all four major tournaments in one year but was beaten in the British Open by Lee Trevino. Jack was the leading money winner on the tour in 1975 when he won the Masters and the PGA. In 1976 Jack was named Player of the Year without winning a major tournament.

Jack has designed 100 golf courses all around the world. His favorite is Muirfield Village in his hometown of Columbus, Ohio. He calls winning the PGA Memorial Tournament at Muirfield in 1977 his greatest victory. Jack has represented the United States in the World Cup competition and won six times (1963, 1964, 1966, 1967, 1971, 1973). He has posted wins in the Senior PGA Tour.

He was named PGA Player of the Year in 1967, 1972, 1973, 1975, and 1976 and won six Masters titles, five PGA Championships, four U.S. Open titles and three British Opens. No other golfer has ever played better for longer than Jack Nicklaus. He is acknowledged by many to be the best golfer in the world.

Suggested Activities and Extensions

1. Read more about golfers who competed against Jack Nicklaus, like Arnold Palmer, Gary Player, Tom Watson, and Lee Trevino. Check the sports sections of the newspapers or read magazines like *Golf Digest* to find out what they are doing today.

2. Jack's concentration on the game has been an important factor in his success. If possible, watch a golf tournament and discuss how the setting encourages player concentration. Apply this to your students' study habits. Do you need quiet to concentrate, or do you prefer to study with music or a television in the background? Do you enjoy watching a golf tournament, or do you need more excitement?

3. Arrange for a class outing to play miniature golf or practice putting competitions in your classroom.

4. It is said that golf is the only sport without umpires or referees. The players are expected to be honorable and report their own strokes and penalties. To do this accurately, of course, requires that each golfer know the rules of the game. Besides the formal rules, golf also has a rather elaborate code of courtesy and etiquette that requires that each person (player or spectator) remain still when another is addressing the ball, refrain from stepping in the line of another's putt, replace one's own divots, etc. Compare and contrast this behavior to that prevalent in many other professional sports. Discuss what this says about golfers in general and how this concept applies to life. Can we trust everyone to be honorable? How would life be different if we could? How might society move toward this goal?

5. Prepare a booklet entitled the Rules of Golf Etiquette. It may be organized in a do-and-don't fashion, illustrated with drawings or stick figures. (The illustrations may be humorous if desired.)

6. Jack Nicklaus has written three instructional books—*Golf My Way,* Simon and Schuster, 1974; *My 55 Ways to Lower Your Golf Score,* Simon and Schuster, 1985; and *Play Better Golf,* Simon and Schuster, 1989. Look at these books and then select an activity that you enjoy doing which has multiple steps. Write the instructions and provide illustrations in sequential order.

7. The most recent golfer of note to rival Jack Nicklaus' early mastery of the game is Tiger Woods. Prepare a comparison chart showing exactly how Woods has surpassed Nicklaus' accomplishments and exactly what achievements remain for him to equal or surpass.

Related Reading

The Junior Golf Book by Larry Hayes and Rhonda Glenn. St. Martin's Press, 1994.

Golf Legends by Bob Italia. Abdo and Daughters, 1990.

Golf Rules in Pictures by United States Golf Association. Perigee, 1988.

PGA Manual of Golf by Gary Wiren. Maxwell Macmillan, 1991.

Golf Course Design

Jack Nicklaus has designed 100 golf courses. There are many ways to arrange the holes from tee to green. Here is an example.

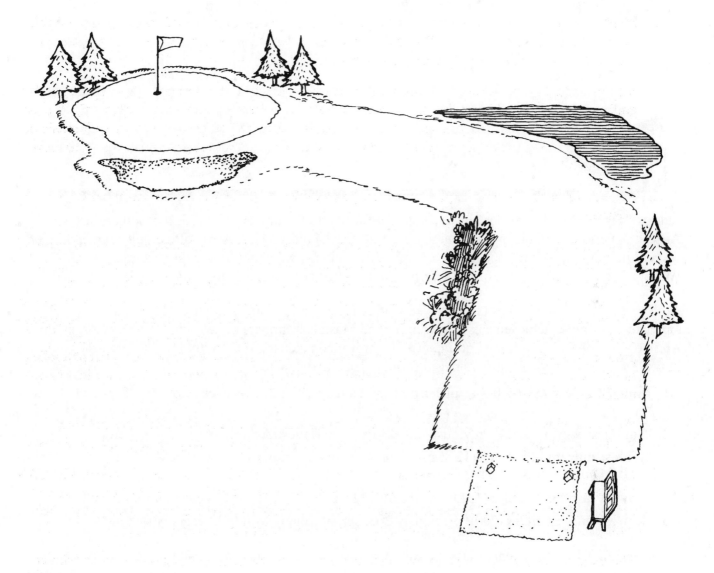

Use the back of this paper to design one hole including the items listed below. When you have finished, work with eight of your friends to design a nine-hole golf course on a large sheet of chart paper.

Make a legend that shows the following:

- **trees**
- **bunkers** (sand traps anywhere between tee and green)
- **fairway** (short grass, the safest direct route to the green)
- **rough** (long grass, on each side of the fairway)
- **water hazard** (anywhere between tee and green)
- **green** (smooth, closely mown grass surrounding the hole)

Tiger Woods

(1975–)

Eldrick "Tiger" Woods was born in Cypress, California, on December 30, 1975. His father Earl is African American, and his mother Kultida is Thai. Earl, a retired U.S. Army officer, nicknamed his son "Tiger" in honor of a South Vietnamese Army officer alongside whom he fought. Tiger attended Western High School in Anaheim, California, and studied at Stanford University from 1994 to 1996.

At the age of 21, Tiger Woods has achieved worldwide fame for some stunning athletic successes. The most recent of these achievements was winning the Masters Tournament held in Augusta, Georgia, on April 10–13, 1997. On a storied golf course, he prevailed against a field of the world's greatest golfers. In those four brief days, he also managed to set at least five new records:

1. **Low 72-hole score** (270—18 under par!) previously set at 271 by Jack Nicklaus 32 years before in 1965
2. **Youngest winner at 21**, previously 23, set by Seve Ballesteros in 1980, 17 years before
3. **Widest margin of victory** (12 strokes), previously nine strokes by Jack Nicklaus 32 years before in 1965
4. **Lowest middle 36 holes** (131), previously 132, set by Nick Price 11 years before in 1986
5. **Lowest final 54 holes** (200), previously 202, set by Johnny Miller 22 years before in 1975

In Woods' first 15 professional starts, he has won four, placed second once, and placed third twice.

Nevertheless, Tiger Woods' performance has not been a complete surprise to those who follow golf. At age 15 he became the youngest player to win the U.S. Junior National Championship and was named *Golf Digest* Player of the Year. At age 16 he became the first player to win the U.S. Junior National Championship twice and was named Titleist-*GolfWeek* National Amateur of the Year. At age 17 he won the U.S. Junior National Championship for a record third time and was named *Golf World* Player of the Year. At age 18 he became the youngest player to win the U.S. Amateur Championship. At 19 he won his second consecutive U.S. Amateur Championship. At age 20 he won the NCAA Championship and became the first player to win three consecutive U.S. amateur titles. He turned professional on August 23, 1996, and immediately signed endorsement contracts with Nike and Titleist for a total of 60 million dollars. At a time when golf is more competitive than ever, Tiger Woods towers over the field like a Colossus. At 21 he has become an athletic hero to millions of people of all races all over the globe.

Suggested Activities and Extensions

1. Tiger Woods consistently outhit his fellow golfers, averaging 330 yards per drive in his 1997 Masters win. This is an impressive distance; yet Woods is lighter and less physically imposing than many of his competitors. Experts say that athletes with superb coordination and timing can many times outperform those with greater bulk and strength. Develop a list of "small" athletes whose exploits have been remarkable. See if you can find one representative from each of the nine fields covered in this book—baseball, basketball, figure skating, football, golf, gymnastics, soccer, tennis, and track and field.

2. Tiger Woods practices hours a day in order to be the best at his game. Is there anything you would be willing to practice eight hours a day? Make a list of activities that students do that require substantial practice time to attain a high level of skill.

3. What do you think it would be like to practice from childhood to be a professional athlete? Discuss the advantages and disadvantages.

4. If possible, visit both a neighborhood public golf course and a country club. Compare the two experiences. Which is a better place to play? Explain. Find out how each course accommodates junior players.

5. The biography on page 64 explained the origin of Tiger Woods' nickname. Greg Norman is known throughout the golfing world as "The Great White Shark." Determine the reasons for this nickname and compare it to Jack Nicklaus' nickname of "The Golden Bear." Discuss the reasons for and functions of nicknames in athletics—as descriptive of the athlete's character, as publicity promotions, as affectionate identities conferred by fans, as sports writers' inventions, etc.

6. Compile a list of athletes and their nicknames, creating a sports nickname book for the class. Following are some well known nicknames to start the ball rolling:

• Champagne Tony	• The Yankee Clipper	• Hammerin' Hank
• Slammin' Sammy	• The Splendid Splinter	• FloJo
• Terrible Tommy	• The Walrus	• The Flying Finn
• The Galloping Ghost	• Big Mama	• The Ice Maiden
• Iron Mike	• The Greatest	• The Carlyle Indian
• Little Mo	• The Brown Bomber	• Dr. J
• Wilt the Stilt	• Dandy Don	
• Air Jordan	• Magic	

Related Reading _____

Golf Basics by Roger Schiffman. Prentice-Hall, 1986.

The Junior Golf Book by Larry Hayes and Rhonda Glenn. St. Martin's Press, 1994.

PGA Manual of Golf by Gary Wiren. Maxwell Macmillan, 1991.

This Place Is Lonely by Vickie Cobb. Walker, 1991. (Australia)

Golf Rules

Here are some things to know before you begin:

1. Be sure you carry no more than 14 clubs in your bag.

2. Put an identifying mark on each of your balls with a marker or pen.

3. After the first hole, the player with the lowest score on the previous hole is given the honor of teeing off first. The condition is known as "having the honor."

4. Play the ball where it lies. Do not touch it unless a rule permits.

5. If your ball goes into a hazard, you may drop it behind the hazard wherever you wish and play again. Add one penalty shot to your score.

6. If you hit a ball out of bounds, hit a new ball from the original position and add one penalty stroke to your score, counting all strokes with both balls.

7. You may remove any objects, natural or artificial, from the line of your putt. However, you may not repair or tamp down any spike marks.

8. When your ball is on the green, you may lift it to clean it. Put a small round marker (usually a coin) down behind the ball so that you will know where to replace it.

9. If you hit the flagstick from the green, there is a two-stroke penalty.

10. You may take practice swings anywhere except in a hazard or bunker.

    • Use these rules and the information in the Nancy Lopez work sheet to design your own Golf Instruction Book.

    • Rewrite the rules in your own words.

    • Choose any three rules to illustrate with diagrams or drawings.

Gymnastics

Gymnastics, as we know it, had its beginnings in Germany. Friedrich Ludwig Jahn, a school teacher, formed the first outdoor gymnasium in 1811. It was a place to practice gymnastics. He believed that gymnastics would strengthen the children of his country. Jahn is considered to be the "father of modern gymnastics." He invented much of the gymnastic equipment used today, like the parallel bars, horizontal bar, balance beam, horse, and the rings.

Europeans brought their love of the sport to the United States. The first program in an American school was begun in 1825 by Charles Beck. A year later, the first college program was begun at Harvard University.

The International Gymnastics Federation was formed in 1881. Men's gymnastics was made an Olympic event in 1896. There are six men's events: floor exercise, pommel horse, still rings, vault, parallel bars, and horizontal bars. The Germans won three of the six events in the first competition. There also is an all-around competition for men today, consisting of all six events. The athlete is to perform a compulsory routine first, followed by an optional routine (whatever movements he desires) in all the events. Present international meets feature all-around gymnasts in competition.

The first world championship was held in 1903, with men competing for all-round and team titles. The modern form of the sport was adopted in 1924. It included a championship for performances on each piece of equipment.

The first women's Olympic participation in gymnastics was held in 1928. The United States did not enter a team until 1936. In the early days, women competed separately in some of the men's events. The 1952 Summer Olympics marked the first recognition of women's gymnastics as a separate sport with its own events. There are four women's events: the vault, uneven bars, balance beam, and floor exercise. As with men, women also have an all-around competition. The athlete performs a compulsory routine first in all four events and then follows it with an optional routine of her choosing. Also as it is with the men, international meets are open only to all-around gymnasts. Rhythmic gymnastics was added to the Summer Olympic Games in 1984. It combines movement with the handling of small equipment like a club, hoop, ribbon, or ball.

Judging in gymnastics is based on form, difficulty, and combinations of movements. Points are deducted for falls, incorrect body positions, stops, leaving out required moves, or excessive slowness. Points may be added for original or exceptionally difficult maneuvers in the original routines. A perfect score is 10. Men's events have five judges, and women's events use seven.

For more information write to the following addresses:

- USA Gymnastics
  Pan American Plaza
  201 South Capitol Ave. Suite 300
  Indianapolis, Indiana 46225

- Gymnastics Hall of Fame
  227 Brooks St.
  Oceanside, California 92054

Nadia Comaneci

(1961–)

Nadia Comaneci was born November 12, 1961, in Onesti, Romania, a small town about 60 miles from the Russian border. Her father was an auto mechanic, her mother a hospital worker. She was six years old when she was discovered by Bela Karolyi, the coach of the Romanian Olympic gymnastics team. Nadia and her friend were pretending to be gymnasts on the school playground when Karolyi and his wife noticed her talent. They visited her parents who agreed to allow Nadia to attend Karolyi's special school for training in gymnastics.

Nadia was a perfect student—talented, eager to please, and enthusiastic about her sport. Her favorite piece of equipment was the uneven parallel bars. Coach Karolyi believed that her best events were the vault and balance beam. Besides gymnastics, Nadia also took ballet lessons to make her more graceful.

By 1975 Nadia was eligible to enter senior international competitions. In her first competition, the European Championships, Nadia placed first in the vault, uneven bars, beam, and all-around. She entered the American Cup in March 1976. Nadia performed the difficult Tuskahara vault perfectly and won the Cup for Romania. At the 1976 Olympics in Montreal, Nadia was on the Romanian team.

Her Olympic scores soon made her name well known to sports fans. Nadia scored a 9.9 on the balance beam and became the first person in Olympic history to receive a perfect score of 10 points on the uneven bars. She also scored a perfect 10 in the individual competition on the uneven bars and the beam. In all, Nadia scored seven perfect 10s in the 1976 Olympics. She also received three gold medals (one in individual all-around), a silver, and a bronze medal for the floor exercises. Her dismount from the uneven parallel bars was named after her (the *Salta Comaneci*).

After the Olympics, Nadia returned to Romania as a heroine. She was awarded a car, a vacation, and a medal of honor from the Romanian government. In 1981, the Karolyis defected to the United States. Nadia assumed the role of coach to the promising gymnastic students of Romania. Then, in November 1989, Nadia decided to defect to the United States and perform with the Olympic All-Stars.

Suggested Activities and Extensions

1. Does anyone in the class take ballet lessons? Ask them to describe what takes place and to talk about the benefits of ballet study. Look at drawings of ballet movements to determine their similarity to gymnastics.

2. Nadia's hobby was collecting dolls from the countries she visited. Discuss the hobbies of your class members. What do they learn from collecting? Ask them to bring their hobbies to share with the class. Encourage them to try a hobby if they have none.

3. Locate Bucharest, Romania, on a map of the world. Research information to learn about the politics of Romania today.

4. Nadia was a very serious gymnast. She practiced diligently. Do you suppose her character traits would have helped her succeed at anything she tried? Explain.

5. Read about Olga Korbut, the Soviet girl who won two gold medals in the 1972 Olympics. She competed against Nadia in the 1976 games. Olga was friendly and outgoing in contrast to Nadia's more serious manner.

6. Women's Olympic gymnastics is scored by seven judges. Each woman starts with a score of 9.4, and the judge adds points, depending on the difficulty of a gymnast's routine. The judges may subtract points for flaws in the routine or missing required moves. The highest and lowest scores are dropped, and the final score is the average of the remaining scores. Compare and contrast this with the scoring of women's figure skating (see Kristi Yamaguchi, page 44).

7. Research the incidence of sports injuries connected with gymnastics. What seem to be the most frequent injuries, the most dangerous events, and the injuries that take the longest to heal? Interviewing coaches and gymnasts will be a good start for this activity. Chart or graph your results.

8. After compiling and charting information on gymnastics injuries, develop a table of safety rules and practices for the sport. Illustrate the recommended practices with drawings. Stick figures are often helpful.

9. Gymnastics is a physically demanding sport. To achieve high degrees of excellence, girls must start training very young, and their peak performances are usually achieved by the early or mid-teens. Then natural changes occur in the girl's weight and center of gravity, along with general shape and configuration. Because of these facts, women gymnasts are rarely, if ever, able to continue a competitive career. What effect does this have on the rest of their lives? Discuss and research the later lives of some well known female gymnasts. What did they do? Were they successful?

Related Reading _____

My Book of Gymnastics: Health and Movement by Amanda Durrant. Wayland Publishers, 1993.
The Olympic Summer Games by Caroline Arnold. Watts, 1991.
Romania by Betty Caran. Childrens Press, 1988.
Step-by-Step Ballet Class: the Official Illustrated Guide, produced by the Royal Academy of Dance.
    Contemporary Books, 1994.
Wonder Women of Sports by Betty Millsaps. Random House, 1981.

Slowly and Gently

Here are some exercises that gymnasts do to keep their bodies in good condition. Match the words and pictures.

_____ 1. Sit with the soles of your feet together. Gently press your knees down to the floor.

_____ 2. Bend your front leg forward and lean your weight onto it.

_____ 3. Stand next to a wall. Put your palms on it. Push off as if you were doing push-ups.

_____ 4. Lie on your stomach. Lift up your head and legs slowly. Arch your back.

_____ 5. Press your palms on the floor and try to straighten your legs.

_____ 6. Put your hands flat on the wall. Keep your back straight. Push your shoulders down.

_____ 7. Lie on your back with your knees bent. Put your hands behind your head and rise up slowly.

_____ 8. Sit on the floor with your legs spread out. Reach as far as you can down your left leg. Repeat on your right side.

_____ 9. Squat down and then jump up as high as possible.

Try these exercises but remember all stretching must be done **slowly** and **gently**.

Fold under.

Answers:

1.—C   2.—E   3.—G   4.—A   5.—D   6.—B   7.—F   8.—I   9.—H

Sawao Kato

(1946–)

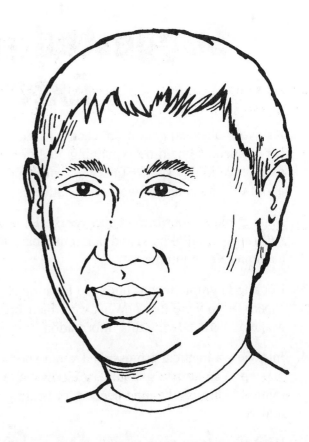

Sawao Kato was born on October 11, 1946, in Nigata, a small town on the island of Honshu. He became interested in gymnastics at age 14. Sawao enrolled in the Tokyo Educational University in 1965 and trained with Akitomo Kaneko, an Olympic veteran gymnast.

He first entered the World University Championships in 1967 and placed third in all-around. He medaled in five individual events. At the 1968 Olympics in Mexico City, Sawao was again the all-around champion. He won a gold medal in the floor exercise and a bronze medal in the rings. The 5' 3", 125-pound gymnast became a part of the "V–10" dynasty, a succession of 10 Japanese teams that won titles in Olympic and World Championship competitions.

Kato had to overcome a bad shoulder and elbow injury to compete in the 1972 Olympics. In Munich, he was among the top six gymnasts in each event and took three individual gold medals as well as the team gold. He was the all-around champion again. Shortly after the Munich Olympics, Sawao was injured in an automobile accident. He missed a year of training.

On April 2, 1973, Sawao was married to Makiko Matsubara. The couple has three daughters. Sawao was back in training and ready to compete in the 1976 Montreal Olympics. He was 29 years old and had problems with his ankle. He was among the top six in four events and won his second gold medal on the parallel bars. Sawao also received his third team gold medal, making him the first gymnast ever to win gold medals in three successive Olympics.

Kato retired after placing fourth in the 1977 World Championships. He was 31 years old. By 1979 he had stopped competing and became a coach at Tsukuba University with his friend and mentor, Akitomo Kaneko. In 1983 he published a manual on gymnastics technique.

Suggested Activities and Extensions

1. Ask your physical education teacher to teach your class some basic gymnastic moves. Ask him or her to spend some time explaining qualities other than physical strength needed for developing excellence in this sport. Talk with your students about their experiences. What did they learn about the characters of world class athletes?

2. Male gymnasts perform in six events. They use these pieces of equipment: the pommel horse, still rings, parallel bars, and horizontal bar. Research information and make detailed drawings of each piece of equipment.

3. Look at Olympic record books to learn more about the other members of the V–10 dynasty from Japan. Who were they? What were their best events? What individual medals did they win? Make a chart showing this information.

4. Interview a medical professional about sports injuries like a torn Achilles tendon. Ask what can happen to an athlete's shoulders, elbows, and ankles. We know that Sawao was frequently injured. Discuss the time needed for healing and precautions an athlete can take to avoid being injured.

5. How much of an average athlete's career is spent caring for injuries? (Clearly, this varies with individuals, but try to determine some sort of trend or generalization that can be made for different sports.) Many physicians advise avoiding continued competitive use of an injured joint, bone, tendon, ligament, or muscle until it has completely healed. Nevertheless, some professional athletes do not follow this advice, continuing instead to compete in spite of their condition. What might be the reasons for such actions? Do you think those reasons are justified or short-sighted?

6. Read more about Sawao Kato's native country of Japan. List five other Japanese gymnasts.

7. Japan has shown an adaptability to other sports which, like gymnastics, are not native to the land or culture. Both golf and baseball have world class athletes who come from Japan. Prepare a class display of pictures and reports on Japanese athletes, men and women, who have gained worldwide fame as individuals.

Related Reading

The Complete Book of the Olympics by David Wallechinsky. Little, Brown, 1991.

Gymnastics by Bob Bellew. Watts, 1992.

Gymnastics by Kate Haycock. Macmillan, 1991.

Gymnastics by Sean McSweeney and Chris Bunnett. B.T. Batsford Ltd., 1993.

The Illustrated History of Gymnastics by John Goodbody. Beaufort Books, 1983.

Journey Through Japan by Richard Tames. Troll, 1991.

World Events

Do historical research to determine five important world events for each of the years that Sawao Kato won Olympic gold medals. These would be, of course, important events in his life, influencing him at the same time that he himself was affecting history. It was a remarkable span of eight years when one man was able to maintain world dominance in one field of athletics.

1968

1. _____
2. _____
3. _____
4. _____
5. _____

1972

1. _____
2. _____
3. _____
4. _____
5. _____

1976

1. _____
2. _____
3. _____
4. _____
5. _____

Shannon Miller

(1977–)

Shannon Miller was born March 10, 1977, in Rolla, Missouri. She grew up in Edmond, Oklahoma. Her father was a college physics professor at the University of Central Oklahoma, and her mother worked as a bank vice president. At just five years of age, Shannon began bouncing on the family trampoline with her sister, Tessa. When she was eight years old, Shannon went to the Soviet Union for a two-week training camp in gymnastics. On returning, she began training six days a week with her coach, Steve Nunno. Besides gymnastics, she studied ballet and jogged every day.

Shannon went to the gym early each morning, attended school, and then returned to the gym until nine P.M. After that, she did homework, played with her pets, and spent time with her family. Shannon maintained a straight A average throughout her high school career and was a member of the National Honor Society. Her hard work began to pay off as she dominated local gymnastics meets and finally became a top international competitor.

In 1988 Shannon placed second in the Pan American Games and first in her age category at the United States Championships. She was on her way to becoming an international star. In 1990 Shannon ranked second at the American Classic and was the best all-around gymnast at the Catania Cup competition in Italy. The next year, she ranked seventh at the U.S. Championships which was won by Kim Zmeskal. She focused all her efforts on the 1992 Summer Olympics. She performed brilliantly (despite elbow surgery) at the Olympic trials and was named one of six members of the U.S. team.

Shannon lost the all-around gold medal to Tatiana Gutsu in the finals. It was the closest loss in Olympic history. She won two silver and three bronze medals, more than any other woman. She returned to Oklahoma a heroine. She was made the honorary mayor of Oklahoma City and honorary governor of Oklahoma. She was given a new car, even though she was too young to drive.

In 1993 she won the all-around competition in the United Championships, the Olympic Festival, and the U.S. Championships. The U.S. Olympic Commission named her Sportswoman of the Year. She is the only woman to have won two all-around titles at the World Championships (1993–1994). Shannon also competed in the 1996 Olympic Games in Atlanta, taking a gold medal for the balance beam and leading the team to a gold medal.

Suggested Activities and Extensions

1. Look in the phone book or contact your local YMCA for gymnastics classes in your area. Invite an instructor to visit your class to talk about conditioning.

2. Read more about Kim Zmeskal, the first American to win the all-around title in the World Championships and a member of the 1992 U.S. Olympic team. What elements of her background and personality are like or unlike the background and personality of Shannon Miller?

3. How do you think Shannon Miller behaved after losing the gold medal to Tatiana Gutsu? How do you think she really felt? Do you think winning second place in an individual sport like gymnastics is different from taking second place in a team sport? Explain. Are you a good loser? (What does the phrase *good loser* generally mean?) How important is sportsmanship in everyday life?

4. Learn more about the Olympics in Atlanta, Georgia, with *Share the Olympic Dream* (TCM 604). What do you think Shannon Miller did to prepare? For her, how was this Olympics different from the previous one in Barcelona, Spain?

5. Write three questions that you would like to ask Shannon Miller. Include them in a fan letter you might send her.

6. At four feet six inches tall and weighing 69 pounds, Shannon was the smallest member of the U.S. Olympic team. Try to find a student who is near that size so you can understand her appearance.

7. Most sports that provide large sums of money for the athletes are ones that generate large spectator crowds. The Olympics are broadcast all over the world, and gymnastics has always been a favorite of the viewers. Why is it that gymnastics has never been a great source of income for the athletes, like skating, golf, tennis, basketball, baseball, and football? Do these sports require more skill? Are they more interesting? More popular? More deserving? Discuss.

Related Reading

The Complete Book of the Olympics by David Wallechinsky. Little, Brown, 1991.

Everybody's Gymnastics Book by Bill Sands and Mike Conklin. Scribner, 1984.

Gymnastics by Bobbie Kalman. Crabtree Publishing Co., 1996.

Gymnastics by Bob Bellew. Watts, 1992.

Gymnastics by Sean McSweeney and Chris Bunnett. B.T. Batsford Ltd., 1993.

Gymnastics: A Step-by-Step Guide by Carey Huber. Troll, 1990.

The Gymnasts (a fiction series) by Elizabeth Levy. Scholastic.

Winning Women by Fred McMane and Catherine Wolf. Bantam, 1993.

Women's Events

Women compete in four events at gymnastic meets. Here they are in order of performance:

The Vault

Women jump over a padded piece of apparatus called a "vaulting horse." They begin with a run and a jump from a springboard which sends them flying into the air. It is important to push off the horse with power because the gymnast performs acrobatic movements while in the air. The gymnast must land with her feet in front, knees bent, and then stretch her arms above her head with her back straight. The vault is scored on height and distance in the air, difficulty of movements, and accuracy of landing. In most competitions, the vault is attempted twice. The highest score counts.

How is the vault scored?_____

_____

The Asymmetric (Uneven) Bars

The uneven bars are made of fiberglass connected by cables. They are 7'9" and 5'2" high. The gymnast performs required moves in a routine that usually lasts about 30 seconds. She swings between the bars quickly and must change directions and hand grips often. Simple dismounts are made from the highest point of the swing with a half turn. The gymnast must land with her feet in front, her knees bent, and stretch her arms above her head with her back very straight.

Describe the appearance of the uneven bars. _____

_____

Balance Beam

The balance beam is 15 feet long, four feet high, and four inches wide. The routine lasts between 70 and 90 seconds. Gymnasts perform a number of difficult moves on the beam, including jumps, turns, leaps, headstands, and rotational exercises. Many of the moves use French names from ballet. Some athletes do somersaults and cartwheels on the balance beam. Scoring is based on the difficulty of the routine, with points being deducted for falls, missteps, imperfect dismounts, or missed elements.

Name five moves that gymnasts do on the balance beam. _____

_____

_____

Floor Exercise

Floor exercises are performed on a mat 40' by 40'. The routine is performed to music and lasts between 70 and 90 seconds. The performer must use the entire mat space. Gymnasts blend elements of dance and athleticism into a graceful program of strength, flexibility, and balance. Scores are based on required elements and artistic expression.

How are the floor exercises different from other gymnastic events?_____

_____

Soccer

To improve their physical fitness, the early Greeks and Romans played games similar to soccer. The Romans introduced the game to the British Isles about 1,500 years ago. These kicking games, very popular in Britain, were played by large groups of people over miles of land. There were no official rules.

By the 1800s the modern game of soccer was being played in many English schools. Rules were written by J.C. Thring in 1862. There are 11 players on a team, including the goalkeeper. The uniform includes short pants, a jersey, rubber-cleated shoes, shin pads, and long socks. The match consists of two 45-minute periods of play. There is one referee who calls fouls on players for violations like bumping another player or handling the ball. He may allow the fouled player a free kick or a penalty kick. If a player is removed from the game, another player is not substituted. Goals are scored by kicking the ball over the goal line into nets on either end of the field.

The London Football Association was formed in 1863. The game became known in England as "association football." That name was shortened to *assoc.* and later to *soccer*, the name most commonly used in the United States. During the late 1800s, soccer was introduced to countries all around the world. It was especially popular in Europe and South America. The Federation Internationale des Football Association (FIFA), formed in 1904, regulates professional soccer all over the world.

The World Cup tournament, held every four years, is the most important international soccer tournament. Each country sends an all-star team of professional players. In 1992, 141 countries competed in preliminary qualifying matches for the month-long event. The winner of the 1994 World Cup was Brazil. The World Cup trophy is kept in Zurich, Switzerland, by the FIFA.

Until recently in the United States, soccer has been played primarily be school-age children. There are now, however, more than 600 college programs. In fact, by the 1990s soccer was recognized as the fastest-growing college and high school sport in the United States. In 1994 it was estimated that there were more than 13 million boys and girls under the age of 18 who played soccer.

A professional league, the North American Soccer League (NASL), was in business from 1968–1985, but soccer has never been as popular in the United States as it has been in other countries. Recently, promoters have formed a new group called Major League Soccer (MLS), hoping to renew interest in professional soccer in the United States.

For more information write to the following addresses:

- U.S. Soccer
  1801–1811 South Prairie Avenue
  Chicago, Illinois 60616
- National Soccer Hall of Fame
  5–11 Ford Avenue
  Oneonta, New York 13820

Diego Maradona

(1960–)

Diego Armando Maradona was born October 30, 1960, in a suburb of Buenos Aires, Argentina. He was one of eight children raised in a poor family, and he spent much of his time playing soccer in the streets. From an early age, Diego showed a great deal of natural talent.

Cesar Menotti, the coach of the Argentine national team recognized Maradona's ability at the age of 15. Even though he was small (5'6"), Maradona, a midfielder, was strong and very fast. He was playing professional soccer by age 16. In 1979 and 1980, he was the South American Player of the Year, and in 1981 his team, the Boca Juniors, won the Argentine League Championship. However, some people criticized Maradona, saying he was not a team player.

After Argentina lost the World Cup to Brazil in 1982, Maradona transferred to play for the Barcelona team in Spain. He stayed there two years before moving to the Napoli club in Italy. By 1986 Maradona had matured as a player and was able to help the Argentine national team win the World Cup. He is considered by many to be the greatest soccer player since Pelé. He was the World Cup Most Valuable Player.

His successes continued with the Napoli team, which won the Italian League championships in 1986, 1987, 1989, and 1990. His career was interrupted when he was suspended from play for 15 months after testing positive for cocaine. During that time, he was also arrested for drug possession. He was unable to play in the 1994 World Cup. Maradona's achievements rank him as one of soccer's greatest players. His skills brought him worldwide fame and wealth, but his future will depend on remaining drug free.

Suggested Activities and Extensions

1. Brainstorm a list of pros and cons of being an excellent individual and/or team player. Which is better? Why?

2. Research more about other famous soccer players—Peter Shilton, Alfredo di Stefano, Franz Beckenbauer, and Michel Platini, for example. Complete the trading card form (page 4) for each one.

3. Learn more about Maradona's native country, Argentina, as well as Barcelona, Spain, and Naples, Italy, where he played professionally.

4. Ask your physical education teacher to show your students how to dribble a soccer ball. (How does the word *dribble* here compare with its use in other sports? Look up this word in the dictionary and explain its origin and various meanings.)

5. Discuss how fame, stress, competition, and wealth may have contributed to Maradona's drug problems. Do you think professional sports teams should have the responsibility of punishing players involved with drugs? Should they have the responsibility of helping players involved with drugs? Are professional athletes necessarily good role models for young people? Explain.

6. Some very bad mob actions have taken place in soccer stadiums, leading to mass injuries, stampedes, and even deaths. These actions have apparently been the result of partisan fan behavior. What are the causes of such behavior? Can violent fan behavior be induced by violence on the field? Are some sports more prone than others to inciting these types of actions? How do you think this kind of destructive violence can be avoided, short of constant police patrols?

7. Develop a booklet of soccer terms with meanings, diagrams, and illustrations. Include some of the following elements:

Referee's signals:
- Warning or Expulsion
- Corner Kick
- Goal Kick
- Indirect Free Kick
- Direct Free Kick
- Penalty Kick

Terms:
- Center
- Charge
- Dribbling
- Drop Ball
- Half-volley
- Volley
- Hands
- Marking
- Obstruction
- Overlap
- Save
- Screen
- Tackle
- Trap
- Heading
- Passing

Related Reading

Argentina by Karen Jacobsen. Childrens Press, 1990.

Soccer: Do You Know the Rules? by J.P. Voorhees. Professional Publications CA, 1994.

Soccer for Boys and Girls: Start Right and Play Well by Bill Gutman. Marshall Cavendish, 1990.

Soccer Techniques, Tactics, and Teamwork by Gerhard Bauer. Sterling, 1993.

The Spectator's Guide to Soccer by Ted Cook. Soccer Publications, 1990

Winning Ways in Soccer by Janet Grosshandler. Cobblehill, 1991.

Soccer Story

Use the following outline to write a story (fiction or news article) about the players on a soccer team.

Soccer Positions

I. **Defenders**
- A. Prevent the opponent from scoring.
- B. Move the ball to the midfielders.
  - 1. Left and right fullbacks play on the outer edges of the field.
  - 2. Stopper (center fullback) stops the other team's striker.
  - 3. Sweeper plays in front of the goalkeeper.
  - 4. Goalkeeper defends his team's goal from the opponents' striker.

II. **Midfielders**
- A. Handle the ball and control the midfield.
- B. Score goals—offensive midfielder sets up plays and scores.
- C. Play defense—defensive midfielder tackles and takes the ball.
- D. Two wings play on the outer edges of the field.

III. **Forwards**
- A. Striker plays closest to the other team's goal.
- B. Withdrawn striker feeds the ball to the striker or scores.

Pelé

(1940–)

Edson Arantes de Nascimento, nicknamed Pelé, was born October 23, 1940, in Minas Gerais, Brazil. His father, Dondinho, was a professional soccer player for a minor league club. He did not earn much money but instilled his love for the game in his son. When Pelé was five years old, his family moved to Bauru, near São Paolo. He did not attend school because the family could not afford tuition. Young Pelé spent much of his time playing soccer in the streets. In those early games, the "ball" was often a bundle of rags, a grapefruit, or an old tin can.

He joined his first organized team, the Bauru Athletic Club at age 13 and became the student of Waldemar de Brito, a superstar of Brazilian soccer. In 1958 at age 17, Pelé was chosen to play on the Brazilian national team at the World Cup in Sweden. He scored six goals and led Brazil to the world soccer championship. On returning, he played for Santos, the most respected team in São Paolo. In that year he scored a total of 87 goals, 58 in league play. Brazil won the World Cup again in 1962, but Pelé missed most of the action because of a muscle pull.

In 1969 Pelé scored his 1,000th goal, and the following year the 30-year-old superstar won his third World Cup with the Brazilian national team. It marked the first time one country had won the world championship three times. Pelé is still the only person to have played on three winning World Cup teams.

Pelé retired from the Santos on October 2, 1974. He planned to leave professional soccer, but within six months he signed to play with the New York Cosmos, a team in the new North American Soccer League (NASL). He attracted many fans, but after three seasons, Pelé retired after a game against his old team, Santos. In that game he played one half with each team. After his retirement, attendance at soccer matches in the United States dropped, and the NASL disbanded in 1984.

Pelé ended his career having played 1,253 games and scoring 1,220 goals. Even in retirement he continues to be a role model for young people. He does not drink or smoke. He is recognized internationally as soccer's greatest player ever.

Suggested Activities and Extensions

1. Pelé was inducted into the Black Athletes Hall of Fame in 1975. Make a list of other athletes probably in the Hall. Sort them by sport.
2. Brainstorm a list of South American athletes. Sort them by country and/or sport.
3. Learn more about Pelé's native country, Brazil.
4. Discuss what it means to be considered the greatest player in the history of the game. Compile a class list of other greatest players by sport. Give three to five reasons to support each of your selections.
5. Take your class out to the playground and draw a soccer field to scale with sidewalk chalk. Mark all the positions, using the diagram on this page to help you.
6. If possible, invite a soccer coach to talk with your students about learning to play the game. Arrange for them to experience passing a soccer ball without using their hands.
7. Create a Venn diagram showing the similarities and differences between soccer and American football. Remember to consider such things as rules, equipment, scoring, terms, maneuvers on the field, etc.
8. The diagram below shows a standard soccer field with an opening line-up that is common but may be changed as the game progresses.

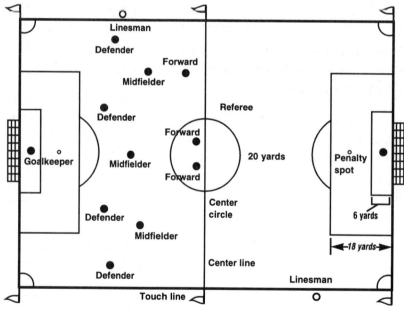

Related Reading

Brazil by Evelyn Bender. Chelsea House, 1990.
Make the Team, Soccer: A Heads-Up Guide to Super Soccer! by Richard Brenner. Little, Brown, 1990.
Modern Soccer Superstars by Bill Gutman. Putnam, 1980.
Pelé, the King of Soccer by Caroline Arnold. Watts, 1992.
Pelé, World Soccer Star by Julian May. Crestwood House, 1975.
Soccer by Paul Joseph. Abdo and Daughters, 1996.
Soccer by Mark Littleton. Zandervan, 1996.
Soccer by Caroline Arnold. Watts, 1991.

Brazil's World Cup

On June 18, 1971, Pelé retired from play with the Brazilian national ream. Thousands of fans wanted him to stay and play another World Cup in 1974. He continued to play for the Santos team for another three years.

If you had been there, what would you have said to try to convince Pelé to continue playing for his country?_____

_____

_____

_____

How do you think Pelé would have responded? _____

_____

_____

_____

After winning three championships, the Brazilian national team won the right to keep the World Cup. Make a drawing of the Cup below and indicate the years of the Brazilian winning games.

The Brazilian national team won the World Cup again in 1994, making it the only country to have won the championship four times. What do you think the newspaper headlines said the morning after the fourth win? On another paper, write a short article that expresses the national pride in their soccer team.

Steve Zungul

(1954–)

Slavisa (Steve) Zungul was born in the city of Split in Dalmatia, Yugoslavia, on July 28, 1954. As a child, he worked with his father, a fisherman on the Adriatic Sea. He began playing in youth soccer tournaments at the age of 11, using a forged document showing his age to be 15. At age 15 he ran away from home for a week to play in another soccer match. When he returned, his angry parents punished him by locking him in his room. By age 17, Steve was signed to the Hajduk Split, a professional team where he stayed six years, scoring 250 goals in 350 games and helping them to win three league championships.

In 1978 he was the leading scorer for the Yugoslavia national team and was named one of Europe's six best forwards by *France Football* magazine. Soon after, Steve came to the United States and met Don Popovic, a former Hajduk Split player who was the coach of the New York Arrows in the Major Indoor Soccer League (MISL). He quickly became involved with this new type of soccer and was very successful. In 18 exhibition games, he scored 43 goals.

With Steven Zungul, the New York Arrows won four successive MISL championships between 1979 and 1982. He became the MISL's all-time leading scorer with 419 goals and 222 assists. He won the Triple Crown in 1980, 1982, and 1985 for the most goals, assists, and points.

Steve is a great natural talent and fierce competitor who says, "I hate to lose; I hate to be beaten at anything." He was able to score with either foot, and his perfect positioning made him a successful rebounder. He was traded in 1983 to the Golden Bay Earthquakes of the North American Soccer League (NASL), allowing him to play outdoor soccer for the first time in five years. When the Golden Bay franchise folded, Steve moved to the San Diego Sockers, a team in the MISL. With his help, they won the 1985 MISL championship. Steve won his sixth MISL scoring title in 1986 with the Tacoma Stars.

He returned to help the San Diego Sockers win the league championship in 1989 and 1990. Following that season, the most successful player in MISL history announced his retirement. He had scored a record 652 goals during his career.

Suggested Activities and Extensions

1. Are there ever any times or circumstances when it is all right to lose? How important is it for a great athlete to be able to accept defeat? Can anyone ever expect to win all the time? Discuss.

2. Learn what you can about Yugoslavia today. Check new encyclopedias for information about the breakup of the country. Locate Dalmatia, Yugoslavia, on an old map.

3. How did Steve Zungul's life change when he came to the United States? What might have happened if he had stayed in Yugoslavia? Name other athletes who have immigrated to the United States. Make a list of the reasons that may have motivated them.

4. Indoor soccer is played on hockey rinks covered with artificial turf. There are six players on a team, and the game lasts for 60 minutes divided into four quarters. Teams are permitted to substitute tired players as long as the ball is in play. Players who commit major fouls are sent to a penalty box as in hockey. Individual ball passing skill is important. Players must make quick decisions because they are playing on a much smaller field. The main effort is in possessing and controlling the ball. Indoor games have much higher scores than outdoor games. There were two indoor leagues—the Major Indoor Soccer League (MISL) and the North American Soccer League (NASL), but both have folded.

   a. Why do you think the indoor soccer leagues failed? Using what you know about soccer, do you think you would have enjoyed attending an indoor game? Why? Why not?

   b. What sports are played successfully indoors and outdoors? What characteristics of these games make that success possible?

5. If you could ask Steve Zungul what he liked most about indoor (as opposed to outdoor) soccer, what do you suppose he would say? (Remember, he was a forward). Write an interview and have pairs of students role-play the questions and answers.

6. How do you think it affects a player to move from one team to another many times? Would this influence his teamwork? His loyalty? His timing? His commitment? How do fans react to players who frequently move or are traded, as opposed to those who remain with one team for an entire career? Discuss.

7. Although the American game is called "football," soccer is a ball game that actually requires more foot skills, especially limiting the use of the hands. Develop a chart showing a comparison of the actual foot moves required in each sport. Use stick figures to illustrate your descriptions.

8. Develop a set of new rules for either indoor baseball or football on an arena such as used for indoor soccer. Make sure to include any changes needed in number of players, equipment, scoring, penalties, positions, times, and substitutions.

9. Design and develop a souvenir program for your soccer team. Include a roster of players, complete with past records, colorful nicknames, and short biographies.

Related Reading

Indoor Soccer Tactics and Skills by Wes Leight. Green Forest Products, 1987.

Tennis

It is believed that the modern game of tennis evolved from an indoor game called "paume" played by the French about 800 years ago. It was really a form of handball. Players used a racket to hit balls over a net, onto ledges around the court, or off walls. The word tennis comes from the French word *tenetz*.

In 1873, a British officer, Major Clopton Wingfield, moved the game outside. Lawn tennis was first played on a court shaped like an hourglass. It was less expensive than court tennis, and the rules were simpler. The game required speed, agility, and the ability to hit the ball with accuracy.

Tennis was introduced in the United States by Mary Ewing Outerbridge of Staten Island, New York, in 1874. News of the game spread, and courts soon opened around the country. In 1881 the United States Lawn Tennis Association was founded, and the first U.S. men's championships were held at Newport, Rhode Island.

The object of modern tennis is to hit the ball over the net and force your opponent to make errors. The server has two chances to put the ball in play. In order to win a game, the player must score four points and win by at least two. Games are organized into sets, and the first player to win six games (by at least two) wins the set. Most matches are decided by winning two out of three sets.

Within 10 years, there were tennis clubs and national championships being played all around the world. Before 1920 all players were amateurs. The first professionals began traveling around the country, earning money from ticket sales. They were not allowed to compete at Wimbledon or for the U.S. championship. In 1968, when officials realized they were not attracting the world's top players, these tournaments adopted an "open" format, permitting both amateurs and professionals to compete together.

There are four major tennis tournaments—the Australian Open, played in Melbourne, Australia, in January; the French Open, played in Paris, France, in May; Wimbledon (the All-England Championships), played near London, England, in June; and the United States Open, played in Flushing Meadow, New York, in late August. They are referred to as the *Grand Slam* events. The Davis Cup is a competition for men's teams around the world, open to both amateur and professional players. Begun in 1900, it has helped make tennis a popular international sport. The Federation Cup, begun in 1963, is a similar international competition for women.

For more information, write to the following address:

> Association of Tennis Professionals
> 200 ATP Tour Blvd.
> Ponte Vedra Beach, Florida 32082

Arthur Ashe

(1943–1993)

Arthur Robert Ashe, Jr., was born July 10, 1943, in Richmond, Virginia. Growing up in the South in the forties, Arthur experienced segregation as a way of life. He was not permitted to play on the city's best tennis courts because of his skin color. Arthur had one brother, John. His mother died when Arthur was just six years old. His father, Arthur, Sr., worked hard to support the family. Arthur helped him clean the grounds of Richmond's biggest playground, Brook Field Park. That experience introduced Arthur to the game of tennis.

His first tennis instruction came from Ron Charity, the best black tennis player in Richmond. Later, Arthur attended tennis camps at the home of Dr. Robert Walter Johnson, a black physician living near Richmond. During his eight summers at this camp, Arthur began competition and in 1955 won both the singles and doubles championships in the American Tennis Association. By 1958, the U.S. Lawn Tennis Association ranked Arthur the fifth top tennis player in the United States under age 15.

He was invited to spend his senior year in high school with Richard Hudlin in St. Louis, Missouri. He was then offered a scholarship to attend the University of California at Los Angeles (UCLA), one of the best tennis programs in the country at that time.

At UCLA, Arthur was the subject of great interest because there had been no great black tennis players since Althea Gibson (women's singles winner, Wimbledon, 1957–1958). As a sophomore, Arthur qualified for Wimbledon. He said that just being there was a dream come true. In 1968 Arthur helped win the first of seven Davis Cup Championships as a member of the United States team.

Arthur Ashe won Wimbledon and the World Championship Tennis tournament in 1975. He married Jeanne Marie Moutoussamy in February, 1977. They had one daughter, Camera. In 1979, Arthur suffered a heart attack and was forced to retire from competitive tennis. During surgery following a second heart attack, it is believed he received a blood transfusion tainted with the AIDS virus. He did not learn that he was HIV-positive until 1988.

Arthur Ashe decided to devote himself to charitable work and writing. He helped establish tennis clinics for minority children in inner cities and became a spokesperson for the American Heart Association. Ashe died of AIDS-related pneumonia on February 6, 1993.

Suggested Activities and Extensions

1. Arthur Ashe grew up in the capital of the old Confederacy. Discuss how this might have affected his determination to succeed, even though he was still restricted by segregation practices in public places such as parks and tennis courts.

2. Learn more about the problems faced by Arthur Ashe when he visited South Africa. Discuss apartheid and the current political situation for the black majority of that country.

3. Read more about another minority tennis star, Pancho Gonzales. Complete the trading card form (page 4) with information.

4. Make a list of characteristics that make Arthur Ashe an outstanding individual as well as a superstar athlete.

5. Research what life was like for black people in the South during the 1940s. Compare and contrast this to life in your area during the same time period.

6. Why was Richard Hudlin important to Arthur Ashe? How do you think his life would have been different if he hadn't met Mr. Hudlin? Discuss why it is important to take advantage of opportunity when it presents itself.

7. Examine old video or film footage of Arthur Ashe playing. Notice the graceful style and smooth strokes of this champion. See if you can compare him with some contemporary player.

8. Interview someone old enough to have seen Arthur Ashe play. Take notes on the remembrances of Ashe's tennis abilities.

9. Richmond, Virginia, Arthur Ashe's hometown, recently erected a statue of the great tennis athlete. The city already has many statues of American historical figures because it was the capital of the Confederacy during the Civil War. Write to the Richmond Visitor's Center for information about Arthur Ashe and the location of his statue. Pretend the statues of Jefferson Davis, Robert E. Lee, and Arthur Ashe come to life. Have them engage in a dialogue about the changes that have taken place in our country since 1865 at the end of that terrible war that killed so many Americans but also put an end to slavery. Write the dialogue in script form and place it in a folder with an appropriately designed cover. Present the dialogue to the class with students reading different parts.

Related Reading _____

Arthur Ashe and His Match with History by Robert Quackenbush. Simon and Schuster, 1994.
Arthur Ashe: Against the Wind by Warren Coleman. Dillon Press, 1994.
Arthur Ashe: Breaking the Color Barrier by David K. Wright. Enslow Publications, 1996.
Arthur Ashe: Tennis Great by Ted Weissberg. Chelsea House, 1991.
Arthur Ashe: Tennis Legend by Jim Spence. Rourke Press, 1995.
Daddy and Me: A Photo Story of Arthur Ashe and His Daughter by Jeanne Moutoussamy Ashe. Knopf, 1993.
Getting Started in Tennis by Arthur Ashe. Atheneum, 1978.
Tennis: Great Star, Great Moments by Andrew Lawrence. G.P. Putnam's Sons, 1976.

Scoring in Tennis

Scoring in tennis is different from other sports. There are several important terms to remember. When a player is serving and cannot get the ball inside the court or over the net, it is called a *fault*. He is allowed to try again, but two straight faults, called a *double fault*, mean he loses a point.

Another term is *love*. Whenever that term is used, it means "zero." The player has not won the point. It takes four points to win a game, but the player must win by at least two points. The first point is called 15. The second is 30, and the fourth point is called 40. Since the server's score is always given first, a score of 30–15, means that the server is leading the opponent 2–1.

If the game progresses to 40–40, it is now at *deuce*. Each additional point is called *advantage*. The official simply says "advantage, Mr. Jones," or "advantage, Ms. Smith," depending on who has won the point. If the player with the advantage point wins the next point, he wins the game. If the opponent wins the next point, the official says the game is "at deuce," indicating a tie. These terms continue until one player wins by two points.

Using what you have read, answer the following questions:

1. Mary and Sue are playing tennis. It is Sue's serve. She has won two points and Mary has won one. What is the score?

   _____

2. Tom and Juan are tied at 40–40. How would the official call the score?

   _____

3. Marcus and Bill are playing tennis. It is Marcus' serve. The score is 40–30. Who must win the next point in order for the game to be over?

   _____

4. Tricia and Bob are playing tennis. Bob is serving. He misses his first serve. He has committed a _____ .

5. Carmen and Joe are playing tennis. Carmen is serving. The score is Carmen 2, Joe 0. What is the score in tennis terms?

   _____

6. Robin and Kate are playing tennis. Kate is serving. They are tied at 40–40. Robin wins the next point. What would the official say?

   _____

Fold under.

Answers:

1. Sue, 30; Mary, 15 2. deuce 3. Marcus 4. fault 5. Carmen, 30; Joe, love 6. advantage, Robin

Bjorn Borg

(1956–)

Bjorn Rune Borg was born June 6, 1956, in Sodertalje, Sweden. As a young boy, his first interest was in ice hockey. He did not try tennis until his father gave him a racket he had won as a prize. The sport appealed to Bjorn, and he spent many happy hours hitting balls against his family's garage wall.

When Bjorn was 11 years old, Percy Rosburg, a nationally known tennis coach, invited him to become his pupil. Bjorn did well with instruction and was the national junior champion by age 13. He left school at 15 to devote his time to tennis. In 1972 Bjorn won the junior title at the Madrid Grand Prix. He also won junior crowns at Berlin, Barcelona, Miami, Wimbledon, and Milan. At 16 he was the world's junior champion.

Bjorn won both his singles matches in the Davis Cup competition. The leader of the Swedish team, Bergelin, became his new coach. With Bergelin's training and lots of hard work, Bjorn became a professional by age 16. Scandinavian Airlines provided money for Bjorn to travel and compete.

His first year on the international circuit was spent refining his game and gaining confidence. He did not win many tournaments. Bjorn first gained the attention of fans and reporters at the 1973 Wimbledon. He was a tennis superstar. Bjorn became the youngest player to win two major international tournaments—the Italian Open and French Open in 1974. A year later, he won five singles titles, including his second French Open and the Davis Cup trophy for Sweden.

In 1976 Borg became the youngest player in 45 years to win Wimbledon. He did not lose a set. He continued to win five consecutive Wimbledon championships (1976–1980). Bjorn Borg was the number one tennis player in the world in 1979. He was the first man to win the French Open four years in a row and six times in all.

By 1983 after 15 years as a professional, Bjorn retired from competition. At age 27, he chose a comfortable life with his family. He became the youngest member of the International Tennis Hall of Fame with his induction in 1987.

Suggested Activities and Extensions

1. Read more about Bjorn's native country, Sweden.

2. To learn more about Bjorn Borg and other tennis pros, write to the following address:

   International Tennis Hall of Fame
   194 Bellevue Avenue
   Newport, Rhode Island 02840

3. Do you believe Bjorn Borg had any regrets about becoming a professional tennis player at such a young age? Discuss the pros and cons of such a decision.

4. Bjorn Borg was the world's junior champion after winning tournaments in Madrid, Berlin, Barcelona, Miami, and Milan. Determine the country and/or state for each of these cities and locate them on a map of the world.

5. Do research to learn other important sporting and current events that occurred during the 1970s.

6. What would you do with your life if you were financially able to retire at 27 years of age?

7. Bjorn Borg's native Sweden has a strongly socialist form of government. Research how this affected Borg's life after he began winning millions of dollars as a tennis star.

8. Sweden, a far northern country, seems a more likely place for developing skiers than tennis players. Nevertheless, the success of one person often acts as a beacon to other young players starting out. Develop a list of other Swedish tennis players who have become world class players since Bjorn Borg established a strong presence in the tennis world.

9. Research a list of Borg's most famous opponents during his long dominance on the courts. (Elie Nastase, Jimmy Connors, etc.) List the titles they won following Borg's retirement.

10. Bjorn Borg was known as a baseline player—that is, he rarely came to the net to volley. His ground strokes were powerful and accurate. Both Jimmy Connors and Elie Nastase had different styles. Locate information about one of these two contemporaries of Borg and write a comparison and contrast of their types of play.

11. Unlike football, hockey, and other violent sports, tennis can be played with skill and enjoyment all through life. Brainstorm a list of other sports that may be enjoyed by all ages and still be considered good activities for physical conditioning. Should schools be emphasizing these types of sports more than they seem to be doing?

Related Reading

Better Tennis for Boys and Girls by George Sullivan. Dodd, 1987.
The Illustrated Rules of Tennis by Wanda Tym. Ideals, 1995.
The Junior Tennis Handbook by Skip Singleton. Betterway Publications, 1991.
Sweden by Donna Bailey. Steck-Vaughn, 1992.
Tennis by Bill Gutman. Marshall Cavendish, 1990.
Tennis: Play Like a Pro by Charles Bracken. Troll, 1990.

The Tennis Court

Tennis courts are 78 feet long. The net divides the court into two halves of 39 feet each. The net is three feet high at the center. The singles court is 27 feet wide. The doubles court is 36 feet wide.

The lines at the ends of the court are called *baselines*. The lines along the sides are called *sidelines*. The net runs across the middle of the court. The line midway between the baseline and the net is called the *service line*. The area between the baseline and the service line is called the *backcourt*. From the center of the service line to the net is the *centerline*, dividing the forecourt into a right and left service court on each side of the net. A player must stand behind his baseline and serve the ball diagonally across the net into the service court box marked by these lines.

Using what you have read, complete the diagram below:

1. Mark the length(s) and width(s) on the tennis court.

2. Draw the net.

3. Label the court with these terms:

   - **baseline**
   - **sideline**
   - **service line**
   - **centerline**

4. Draw two players in position on the court. Use a dotted line (from either player) to show a good serve.

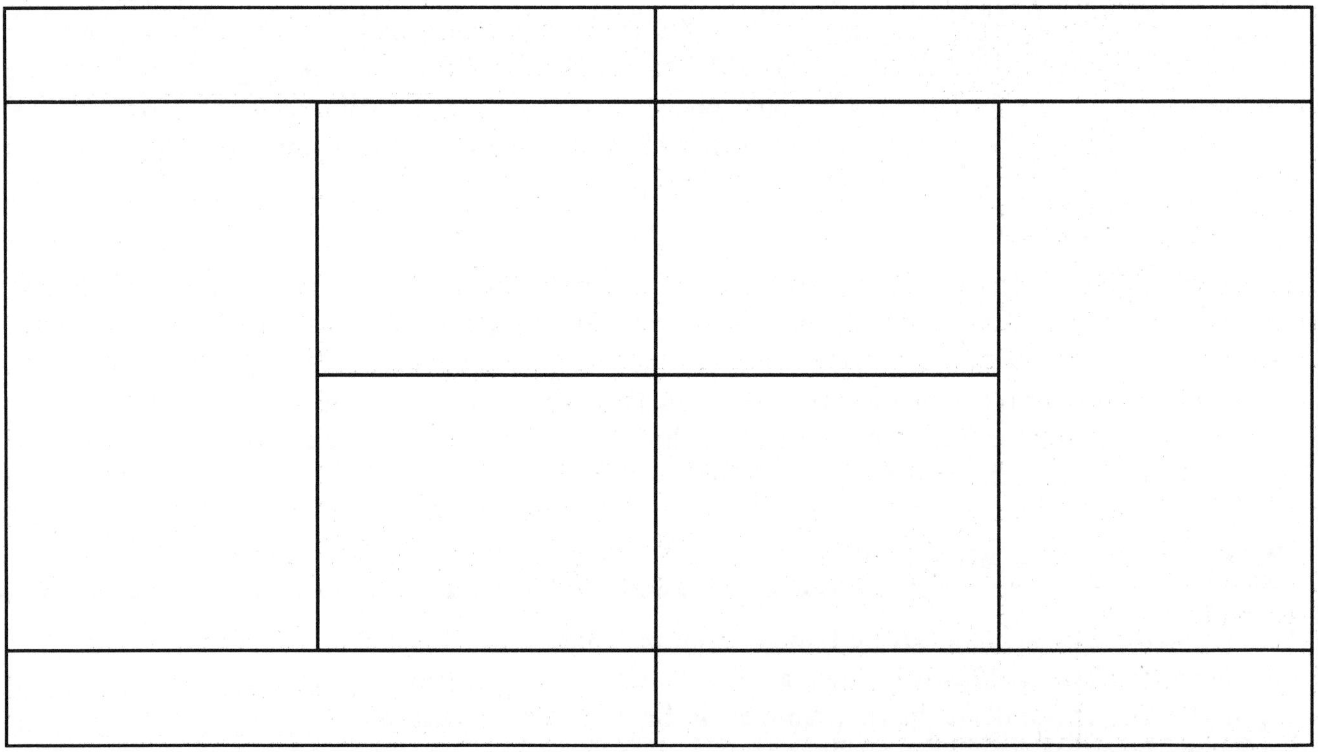

To the teacher: Allow your students to draw and label a scale model of a tennis court on the school grounds. They will need chalk and measuring tapes.

Steffi Graf

(1969–)

Steffi Graf was born June 14, 1969, in Bruhl, Germany. She became interested in tennis at the age of three when she noticed her father's racket. Her father, Peter, was a nationally ranked tennis player, and her mother, Heidi, worked at the tennis club owned by the family. Peter became Steffi's first coach. She won her first junior tournament at age six, and by age 13, she was the German Junior Champion.

Because she had a powerful forehand and a slicing backhand, amateur tennis was not challenging for her. Steffi quit school and entered professional tennis at age 14. She completed her education with a tutor and by mail. Steffi quickly proved that she was capable of professional play by reaching the quarter-finals at Wimbledon. She was the youngest and best player at the 1984 Summer Olympics, where tennis was a demonstration sport. In 1985 she made it to the semifinals of the U.S. Open by defeating Pam Shriver.

Her father continues to have a strong influence on her career. She works very hard and does not allow time for many social activities like dating. On the tour, Steffi prefers to stay with her family and limit association with the other players. She relaxes by reading and listening to music. She maintains a regular training routine which includes running, jumping rope, and lifting weights.

In 1987 Steffi won 11 tournaments, but 1988 was her greatest year in tennis. She won the Grand Slam, winning the Australian Open, the French Open, Wimbledon, and the U.S. Open, and defeating great players like Martina Navratilova, Chris Evert Lloyd, and Gabriela Sabatini. She became the first woman in history to win the French Open without losing a single game. Also that year, Steffi won a second Olympic gold medal.

Between June 1989 and May 1990, Steffi won 66 matches. She lost the top ranking in 1991 because of an injury and family problems but came back to win the 1991 Wimbledon championship. She has now been on the pro tour for 12 years and made millions of dollars through tournament play and endorsements.

Suggested Activities and Extensions

1. Read more about Steffi's native country, Germany. How might the political changes of the last few years affect her career?

2. Read more about Steffi's opponents—Chris Evert Lloyd, Gabriela Sabatini, and Monica Seles. Complete a trading card from (page 4) with information about each of them.

3. In order to build up stamina, a tennis player must do aerobic exercises like running or jumping rope. They also need to do stretching exercises for the muscles of their arms, legs, and back. Invite the school physical education teacher to show your class some stretching exercises appropriate for tennis conditioning. He or she may also discuss weight training to strengthen the wrists and forearms.

4. Even sports that have no body contact, seem to produce their share of injuries. Research the most common sports injuries incurred by tennis players (e.g., what is "tennis elbow"?). Are there any long-term harmful effects that stem from playing this game? If so, what are they and how does one protect against them?

5. Locate the four tournaments of the Grand Slam:
    *   Australian Open, Melbourne, Australia
    *   French Open, Paris, France
    *   Wimbledon, London, England
    *   United States Open, Flushing Meadow, New York

6. Compare and contrast your education with Steffi Graf's. Do you believe it was necessary for her to have private tutors? What did she miss by not attending school? How would you feel about going to school with a professional athlete?

7. Look for Steffi Graf (or other tennis stars) in product endorsements. Share the information with the class.

8. Steffi Graf has been known for her crushing forehand and slicing backhand. Ask a high school tennis team player or coach to come demonstrate how to hit these shots. Have the class practice these shots against a backboard.

9. Ask a skilled player to demonstrate to the class how to serve consistently. (The toss is often a key ingredient to this stroke.)

10. Divide the class into teams and try having a doubles tournament as a culmination activity. Sometimes a "Cardiac Classic" tennis match that features teachers against students is lots of fun.

Related Reading _____

The Olympic Summer Games by Caroline Arnold. Watts, 1991.
Steffi Graf by Judy Monroe. Crestwood House, 1988.
Steffi Graf by Laura Helgers. Sports Illustrated, 1991.
Total Tennis: A Complete Guide for Today's Player by Peter Burwash and John Tullius. Macmillan, 1989.
West Germany by Martin Hintz. Childrens Press, 1983.
Wimbledon by Nancy Gilbert. Creative Education, 1990.
Winning Women by Fred McMane and Cathrine Wolf. Bantam, 1993.

Hitting a Forehand Stroke

Before you can hit a forehand shot, you must grip the racket correctly. The easiest grip is made by shaking hands with the racket. The palm of your hand should always be behind the racket as your arm moves forward in the forehand stroke. This will give you the best control of the ball.

You also need to know the best way to stand while waiting for your opponent's serve. Face the net with your feet slightly apart. Use your nonhitting hand to support some of the weight of the racket. Bend your knees slightly and keep your weight over the balls of your feet. This is called the *ready position* because the player is ready to move in any direction to get to the ball.

The hitting motion of the forehand actually begins with a backswing. The racket should be straight up and down, your elbow close to the body, and your wrist firm. The shoulders turn sideways and the weight is on the right foot. Swing the racket forward, keeping your eye on the ball. A right-handed player will step into the ball on his left foot. The racket should be straight up and down when it hits the ball. After you have hit the ball, be sure to follow through, completing the stroke and giving direction to the ball. After completing the forehand stroke, you should return to the ready position.

Answer the following questions:

1. What two things must you know before you are ready to hit a forehand stroke? _____ and _____

2. Describe each body position when the player is ready.

    - face:

    - feet:

    - knees:

    - nonhitting hand:

3. Number the pictures to show the order of the forehand stroke.

- -

Fold under.

Answers:

1. correct grip; the best way to stand 2. face—looking at the net; feet—apart; knees—slightly bent; nonhitting hand—supporting weight of the racket

Martina Navratilova

(1956–)

Martina Navratilova was born October 18, 1956, in Prague, Czechoslovakia. Her stepfather taught her to play tennis as a young child. As her first coach, he encouraged her aggressive form of play. She entered her first tournament at age eight. In 1968 Russians invaded Czechoslovakia, and life became difficult for Martina and her family because they did not want to join the Communist party. Martina busied herself with school and playing tennis, soccer, and ice hockey.

Martina first visited the United States in 1973 as a member of the Czech Tennis Federation. Because Czechoslovakia was a Communist country, the police were suspicious of her travels and forced her to give much of her earnings to the government. Martina wanted to be free to choose where she would play and how she would use her money. She asked for political asylum in the United States while playing at the 1975 U.S. Open at Forest Hills, New York. So began the career of one of the greatest female tennis players in the world.

After adjusting to her new life in the United States, Martina realized she needed to be more serious about her career. She met Sandy Hanie, a professional golfer who agreed to become her agent. Sandy suggested a training schedule and diet that helped Martina lose weight. In 1978 Martina defeated Chris Evert for the women's singles title at Wimbledon, the first of her nine Wimbledon singles crowns between 1978 and 1990. She was reunited with her family at the 1979 Wimbledon.

Still she did not commit herself to practicing and dropped to number three in the world. It was her friend Nancy Lieberman, a professional basketball player, who convinced her to push herself and build her strength. With Nancy as her trainer and Dr. Robert Haas as nutritionist, Martina began a rigorous schedule of running, weightlifting, and basketball. She stopped eating junk foods and most meats. She hired Dr. Renee Richards, a former tennis pro, as her coach. Her energy and her game soon improved. She was confident and determined to be the best in the game. Martina became a U.S. citizen in 1981.

With the help of her personal coach, nutritionist, and trainer, Martina posted a tournament win record of 98–3 by 1982. She won the U.S. Open in 1983, 1984, 1986, and 1987. Between 1983–1984 she posted a record 74-match winning streak. Martina was clearly the best women's player in the world. She has won 166 singles titles and 163 doubles titles, the most ever by a professional tennis player.

Suggested Activities and Extensions

1. Martina Navratilova has 329 tournament wins in a long professional career. How do you think she would answer these questions?

   - Which was your greatest win? Why?

   - Is winning still exciting, or have you become used to it?

   - What do you do after winning a match? losing?

   - What advice can you give young tennis players?

   Choose one and write a response.

2. Martina Navratilova is a native of Czechoslovakia. Research information about the Czech Republic in a new encyclopedia. How would her career have been different if she had not defected to the United States?

3. For more information about women tennis professionals, write to the following address:

   > Women's Tennis Association
   > 133 First Street, Northeast
   > Saint Petersburg, Florida 33701

4. Read more about the professional careers of two other women tennis players—Martina's coach Billie Jean King and her doubles partner, Pam Shriver. Complete a trading card form (page 4) for each of them.

5. Do you think that having natural talent is enough? How does Martina Navratilova's career prove that hard work is necessary to become successful in sports? Relate this concept to other areas of life—for example, musicians, artists, dentists, policemen, beauticians, etc.

6. Strength and stamina clearly were important requirements in Martina Navratilova's training regimen. Research the rule change in tennis that produced the "tiebreaker" procedure used today. Does today's game require more or less stamina and strength than the older version? Explain. Is today's game the better or the worse for the rule change?

7. Martina Hingis is a leading player among women on the tennis circuit today. She is from Switzerland and was named for Martina Navratilova. Locate information about this great young athlete and list her tournament wins and trophies. Make a chart showing in what ways she is emulating the great Navratilova and what achievements remain for the young namesake if she wishes to match her famous tennis hero.

Related Reading

Martina Navratilova by Jane Leder. Crestwood House, 1985.

Martina Navratilova: Tennis Power by R.R. Knudson. Viking, 1986.

Wimbledon by Nancy Gilbert. Creative Education, 1990.

Welcome to Wimbledon

Wimbledon is the oldest and most prestigious tennis tournament in the world. It is held at the All-England Lawn Tennis and Croquet Club in Wimbledon, a suburb of London, for two weeks every summer. To preserve tradition, the matches are played on grass, and the competitors wear mostly white clothing.

Tournament play is broadcast around the world. Tickets are always sold out as soon as they become available. Spectators enjoy tennis at its finest and a traditional snack of strawberries and cream. They may also visit a museum on the premises, which traces Wimbledon history. Members of Britain's royal family often attend and are seated in the royal box at center court.

Arthur Ashe, Bjorn Borg, Steffi Graf, and Martina Navratilova are all Wimbledon champions. They have all agreed that it is the most important and thrilling tournament victory in the tennis world. Martina has said, "I think I could lose all my other matches throughout the year, but if I still won Wimbledon, I'd be happy."

1. Write the following list of words in alphabetical order and use a dictionary to find definitions for each:

   - tournament
   - prestigious
   - suburb
   - tradition
   - competitor
   - spectators
   - premises
   - broadcast
   - ace
   - volley

Alphabetical Order	Definition

2. Have you ever attended a tennis tournament or watched one on television? Write about the experience on the back of this page.

3. Brainstorm a list of other famous sporting events, such as for football—the Super Bowl; for baseball—the World Series, etc. Attach your list to this page.

Track and Field

Organized track and field competitions began with a sprint race at the first Olympic Games in 776 B.C. at Athens, Greece. Other field events, like the javelin, discus, and long jump were added to the Games until 393 A.D. when Emperor Theodosius of Rome stopped the Olympics for religious and political reasons.

Modern track and field took shape in England in the 1800s. In 1864, Oxford and Cambridge Universities competed in the first track-and-field meet between colleges. By 1880, the sport had become popular in the United States. The Olympics were begun again in 1896 by Baron Pierre de Coubertin of France as a way to promote international friendship through athletics. The performances of early Olympians like Paavo Nurmi (Finland) and Babe Didrikson Zaharias (United States) helped make track and field popular around the world.

Track events all involve running races, from sprints (50–400 meters) to middle distance races (800–5,000 meters) to long distance races (10,000 meters to the 26.2 mile marathon). Some athletes, called ultra-marathoners, compete in 50-mile or 100-kilometer road races. A few even run as many miles as they can in one day. Field events involve jumping and throwing and include the high jump, long jump, pole vault, shot put, discus throw, hammer throw, and javelin.

Athletes may also compete in multi-event sports—the decathlon (10 events) for men and the heptathlon (seven events) for women.

Both these events place emphasis on stamina and versatility. In short, they require the highest order of athletic talent. The decathlon requires two days and includes four track events (100-meter sprint, 400-meter sprint, 110-meter high hurdles, 1500-meter run) and six field events (long jump, shot put, high jump, discus throw, pole vault, and javelin throw). The heptathlon also requires two days and includes three track events (200-meter hurdles, 200-meter run, 800-meter run) and four field events (shot put, high jump, long jump, and the javelin throw). The winners of the decathlon and heptathlon are the ones who accumulate the highest number of points, thus being judged the best all-around athletes, not necessarily the best in each event.

Track and field in America and Europe was originally a sport for amateurs. Athletes had to work to earn a living and were only able to train in their free time. Over the years, this has changed so that many athletes now have corporate sponsors to cover their travel and living expenses. They are permitted to win prize money and earn additional money endorsing products connected to their sport. They are able to be full-time athletes.

The most important track and field competitions are the Summer Olympics and the International Amateur Athletes Federation (IAAF) world championships. Athletes compete in outdoor and indoor track seasons (the USA/Mobil Grand Prix circuit), earning points and winning money based on performance totals.

For more information, write to the following address:

> USA Track and Field
> National Track and Field Hall of Fame
> P.O. Box 120
> Indianapolis, Indiana 46206

Jackie Joyner-Kersee

(1962–)

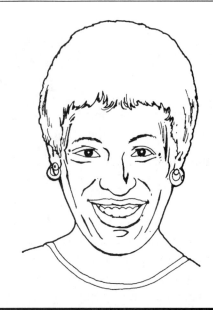

Jackie Joyner was born March 3, 1962, in East St. Louis, Illinois. She was named after President Kennedy's wife, Jacqueline, because her great grandmother predicted she would become the first lady of something—someday. She was the second of four children. Her father had to leave East St. Louis to find work, so her great grandmother helped out at home. Her mother insisted that all her children study hard and have good manners. She wanted them to go to college and work their way out of poverty.

Jackie became involved in track and field at the Mary E. Brown Community Center near her home. Coach Fennoy remembers that Jackie had "the gift," meaning the right mental and spiritual attitude as well as natural talent. He encouraged his students to be well rounded athletes, and because she could run and jump, suggested she compete in the pentathlon. In 1976 Jackie competed in the National Junior Olympics and won her first of four national championships. In high school she was the captain of the track, basketball, and volleyball teams. Upon graduation, Jackie accepted a basketball scholarship to the University of California at Los Angeles (UCLA) with the understanding that she would also compete for the women's track and field team.

While at UCLA, Jackie met coach Bob Kersee. They were married in 1986. With Bob she devoted herself to training for the heptathlon, which includes seven events—shot put, javelin throw, long jump, high jump, 100 meter hurdles, and 200- and 800-meter runs. In 1984 she entered her first Olympics and won a silver medal. At the Goodwill Games in 1986, Jackie set six personal records. Later that year, she received the prestigious Sullivan Award as the country's most outstanding amateur athlete.

Jackie went to the 1988 Olympics in Seoul, Korea, and won a gold medal in the heptathlon. Her coach believes she could have broken the world record for long jump if she had concentrated on one sport, but Jackie prefers the heptathlon because "it shows you what you're made of." When she returned to Los Angeles, Jackie was asked to endorse products like McDonald's and Adidas and to appear on television talk shows. *Sporting News* named her Woman of the Year in 1988. She returned to East St. Louis and spoke with young people about the rewards of hard work and staying drug free. She and Bob established the Jackie Joyner-Kersee Community Foundation to help poor urban young people.

In the 1992 Olympics she again earned a gold medal in heptathlon and a bronze in the long jump. She also competed in the 1996 Olympics in Atlanta, Georgia. Jackie's success is proof that hard work and positive thinking can make dreams come true.

Suggested Activities and Extensions

1. Jackie's brother, Al Joyner, was also a successful track and field athlete, winning a gold medal for the triple jump in the 1984 Olympics. He married Florence Griffith Joyner, an Olympic sprinter. Both women are now coached by their husbands. Discuss the pros and cons of being involved in such a competitive family. Research more about Flo Jo's accomplishments.

2. Jackie is bothered by chronic asthma. Learn what you can about the condition by talking with a health professional or an affected student. How might having asthma affect Jackie's practice and performance?

3. Jackie's record long jump was 24 feet 5 ½ inches. Measure and mark that distance in a grassy area of the playground and invite your students to practice long jumps. Compare their jumps with Jackie's.

4. What is your dream for the future? How do you plan to achieve that dream? What characteristics make some people high achievers? How important is attitude to achievement?

5. Make a list of women track and field athletes. Classify them by their main events.

6. In track and field sports, distance runners seem to reach their prime or peak effectiveness and skill at a later age than do sprinters. Why is this so? Interview coaches, sports doctors, trainers, and physical education teachers for explanations. Have small groups prepare comparison displays showing pictures of the two types of runners with accompanying records of ages, champions, and world and Olympic records for the various distances.

7. Ask a sports psychologist to address the class on different approaches to different events in track and field. Sample questions to explore might be the following:

   - Does the hurdler face the same type of challenge as the sprinter? Does the javelin thrower need the same mind-set as the marathoner?

   - How does the challenge of the pole vault differ from that of the shot put?

   - What is the best mental preparation for a relay runner?

   - How does an athlete overcome the feeling that another competitor is "better" than he or she is?

   - Is it better to run against a clock or against a competitor? Do different competitors respond differently to these two situations?

   - How does mental imaging prepare one for a competition? Is there any evidence that this technique really works?

   - Can sports psychology be applied to good effect in other challenging aspects of our lives— e.g., achieving career goals, overcoming handicaps, learning difficult subjects, studying for tests, etc.? How?

Related Reading

Jackie Joyner-Kersee by Neil Cohen. Little, Brown, 1992.

Jackie Joyner-Kersee, Superwoman by Margaret Goldstein and Jennifer Larson. Lerner, 1994.

Superstars of Women's Track by George Sullivan. Putnam, 1981.

"Three D's"

Jackie Joyner-Kersee credits the "Three D's" for her success as an athlete.

1. Write the definition and give a real-life example illustrating each of the following words:

Dedication

Definition	Real-Life Example

Desire

Definition	Real-Life Example

Determination

Definition	Real-Life Example

2. What is your dream for the future?

   _____

   _____

3. What will you do to achieve that dream?

   _____

   _____

4. Which of the "Three D's" is most important to your success? Explain.

   _____

   _____

Carl Lewis

(1961–)

Frederick Carlton Lewis was born on July 1, 1961, in Birmingham, Alabama. Two years later, his family moved to Willingboro, New Jersey, near Philadelphia, where both his parents worked as high school track coaches. Carl had a typical middle-class childhood; however, he was not as athletic as his brothers and sisters. He had a newspaper route and took cello and drum lessons.

Carl became interested in track after meeting Jesse Owens in 1971. He worked with his parents to improve his skills and within two years placed first in long jump at an Owens track meet. By graduation, Carl was the top ranked high school track athlete in the United States. Carl chose to attend the University of Houston and work with coach Tom Tellez. They became lifelong friends. In 1980, Carl and his sister Carol qualified for the United States Olympic teams but did not compete because the United States boycotted the games in Moscow as a protest against the invasion of Afghanistan. Carl received the 1981 Sullivan Award as America's best amateur athlete.

He was the first athlete since Jesse Owens who had excelled in both track and field events. By the end of 1983, Carl had made 14 long jumps of 28 feet or more. During sprints he often chose to lag just behind his competitors for about half the race and then surge ahead of them to the finish line. At the 1983 U.S. National Championships, Carl won three events—the long jump, and the 100- and 200-meter races. A week later, he won three gold medals at the World Track and Field Championships.

Lewis won four gold medals in the 1984 Olympics for the 100-meter race, 200-meter race, 400-meter relay, and the long jump. Jesse Owens was the only other track and field athlete to perform as well. Carl continued to dominate his sport in world competition. He won two golds and a silver medal in the 1988 Olympics. The gold medal for the 100-meter race was originally awarded to Canadian Ben Johnson, who was later disqualified for drug use.

The best race of Lewis' career came in 1991 at the World Track and Field Championships. He ran the 100-meter sprint in the world record 9.86 seconds. The next year, Carl won two more Olympic gold medals in the long jump and 400-meter relay. With eight Olympic gold medals plus the one he won for the long jump in 1996, Carl Lewis is clearly the greatest track-and field-athlete ever.

Suggested Activities and Extensions

1. Carl has anchored 10 of the U.S. Olympic relay teams. Organize relay races for your class. They will need four people on a team, a baton to pass, and a 400-meter track. Spend some time practicing the passing of the baton. Relay races require not just one's individual best but also good teamwork, timing, and coordination with the baton.

2. Write a conversation that Jesse Owens and Carl Lewis might have had after one of Carl's record-setting performances. Be sure to include facts about the distances and times of both athletes in similar events. Have two students read the conversation aloud.

3. Use a stop watch to measure 9.86 seconds. Carl Lewis ran 100 meters in that amount of time. What can you do in less than 10 seconds? How far can you run?

4. Read information about Bob Beamon, the man who recorded a long jump of 29' 2 $\frac{1}{2}$." Complete a trading card form (page 4) telling what you learned.

5. How might Carl Lewis' life have been different if his parents had not been track coaches? What if they had been lawyers? Or teachers? How important are parents' careers in determining the career choices of their children?

6. Carl Lewis not only won eight Olympic gold medals but he won them over a span of eight years. Few athletes are able to dominate the world (particularly in a sport so dependent on strength and speed as track and field) over such a long period of time. What are the necessary qualities— physical, mental, and moral—needed for this kind of extraordinary effort? Discuss and develop a list of such qualities. As a companion to this list, research what other athletes have ever been able to match such a record.

7. Most school tracks have been built in an oval, the grassy infield part being used for field events like high jump, pole vault, shot put, etc., as well as for team sports such as football and soccer. A standard length for one circuit of many such tracks has been a quarter-mile or 440 yards. Standard American sprints such as the 100-yard dash, 220, and 440 dashes and hurdles were easily measured on these courses. As a group or class project, build a scale model of such a track, marking off the international metric distances of 100 meters, 200 meters, 400 meters, and 1500 meters (showing the number of laps required). In the infield, illustrate the positions for runways, sandpits, etc., for the long jump, high jump, pole vault, shot put, discus, and triple jump.

   (The javelin is generally not included in track events below college level, owing to the possibility of serious accident.)

Related Reading _____

Carl Lewis: Legend Chaser by Nathan Aaseng. Lerner, 1985.

Running the Relay

An Olympic relay is run on a 400-meter track divided into 100-meter lengths. Each team has four members. The lead runner sprints 100 meters before the baton is exchanged within a 20-meter passing zone. During the exchange, the lead runner becomes the trailing runner as he approaches and passes the baton. The second runner then takes the lead. This plan continues through the four team members. They try to pass the baton at full running speed without losing a step. If the baton is dropped, the team has lost. The first team to finish is the winner.

Answer the following questions:

1. How many members are on an Olympic relay team? _____

2. How long is the track? _____

3. How long are the passing zones? _____

4. What do the runners pass? _____

5. What happens if the baton is dropped? _____

In the space below, draw a picture of the 400-meter track. Divide it into fourths and mark the passing zones. Draw a runner at the beginning of each lane. The first runner should be holding a baton.

Mark off a 200-meter length on the playground. Include a 20-meter passing zone. Permit students (working in pairs) to practice passing the baton. Remember to try passing at running speed. Discuss what skills are learned from this activity (cooperation, coordination, concentration, etc.)

Fold under.

Answers:

1. four 2. 400 meters 3. 20 meters 4. a baton 5. the team loses

Jesse Owens

(1913–1980)

James Cleveland Owens was born on September 12, 1913, in Oakville, Alabama. His parents were sharecroppers who worked the farmland of Albert Owens in exchange for the use of a house and the money from half the crop. J.C. (as he was nicknamed) was the youngest of 10 children. In 1920, the family moved to Cleveland, Ohio, on the advice of Lillie, one of J.C.'s sisters, who had gone there and found work.

J.C. attended Bolton Elementary School. He was given the name "Jesse" by a teacher who misunderstood his response to a roll call. Jesse was an energetic and inquisitive student who enjoyed his school, friends, and life in the big city. At Fairmount Junior High he met Minnie Ruth Solomon, who later became his wife. Her parents had been sharecroppers in Georgia, so the pair found that they had much in common. While at Fairmount, Jesse began running track and was coached by Charles Riley. "Pop" Riley set up a training schedule for Jesse, and soon it became apparent that he would develop into a fine sprinter and jumper. In 1930 Jesse entered East Technical High School where he continued his track and field career. At the end of his senior year, Jesse won four medals at the National Interscholastic Championship in Chicago.

While attending Ohio State University, Jesse began preparing for Olympic competition. He qualified for the 1936 Olympic team in the 100-meter and 200-meter sprints as well as the long jump. The Games were held in Berlin, Germany, prior to World War II. Adolf Hitler was intent on proving German supremacy, but Jesse tried to remain above the politics. He achieved his dream by winning gold medals in the 100-meter, 200-meter sprints, long jump, and 400-meter relay. He broke Olympic records in all four events. Jesse Owens became a hero to sports fans around the world.

In 1950 Jesse was named the greatest track and field athlete in history by the Associated Press. After that honor, he devoted most of his time to public speaking and travel. Jesse made a great deal of money from endorsements. He worked as the running coach for the New York Mets and as consultant to the U.S. Olympic Committee. In 1972 Jesse received an honorary doctorate of athletic arts degree from Ohio State University. In 1979 he was diagnosed with lung cancer caused by a lifetime of smoking cigarettes. Jesse Owens died in Tucson, Arizona, on March 31, 1980. He is honored with memorials at Ohio State University, Cleveland, Ohio; Oakville, Alabama; and Berlin, Germany.

Suggested Activities and Extensions

1. Civil rights were a concern for Jesse Owens during World War II (1936 Olympics) and the Vietnam War (1968 Olympics). Explain those events and his response to them.

2. Jesse once remarked that being an Olympic athlete meant training for years for something that is over in seconds. Explain the meaning of that statement. What character traits prepare someone for winning a gold medal?

3. Do additional research about Jesse Owens and make a time line to show the important events in his life.

4. Brainstorm a list of careers that relate in some way to the skills of a track-and-field athlete. Which ones would have been a good choice for Jesse Owens?

5. If you were put in charge of the national physical fitness program, what activities and exercises would you recommend? Make a list of activities and exercises and include information about the benefits of each one.

6. Jesse Owen's coach, Charles Riley, was very important to his success in track and field. Discuss how responsible adults can be a positive influence on the lives of young people.

7. Nutrition plays a large part in the life of an athlete. What special nutritional practices should be followed by track-and-field athletes? Are these any different from the practices that should be followed by everybody? Why or why not? Reproduce a copy of the food triangle showing the major groups of foods and daily servings recommended for each.

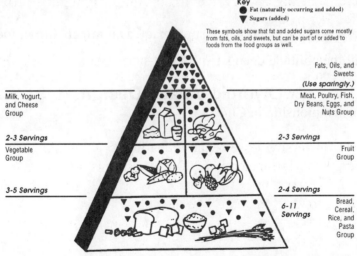

8. Prepare a week's menu for an athlete in training for a track meet. Consult a coach or nutritionist for advice.

Related Reading

Jesse Owens by Tony Gentry. Grolier, Inc., 1990.
Jesse Owens by Mervyn Kaufman. Crowell, 1973.
Jesse Owens, Champion Athlete by Rick Rennett. Chelsea House, 1992.

The 1936 Olympics

The eleventh Olympic Games were held in Berlin, Germany, three years after Adolf Hitler came to power. The Nazi regime wanted to use the international competition to prove that German athletes were superior. Hitler ordered that all the German athletes were to be native-born, white, and non-Jewish. The Germans were the first to build an Olympic Village to house the athletes near the city.

When Jesse Owens broke the world record in the 100-meter run, he became an instant sensation. The German people loved him. Hitler was furious that a black man had been successful and refused to shake Jesse's hand at the medal ceremony. Hitler believed that all races were inferior to the blond, blue-eyed Aryan (Germans).

While in Berlin, Jesse made friends with German long jumper Luz Long. The two men had a great deal in common. They were competitors for the gold medal in the long jump but cheered for each other. Although Long was an Aryan, he did not believe in white supremacy. He was the first to congratulate Jesse for his Olympic record long jump of 26 feet, 5 5/16 inches.

Choose one of the following activities:

1. Do research to compile a list of 1936 Olympians, their medals, and native countries.

2. Read more about the anti-Semitic movement in Germany before World War II.

3. What do you think would be needed to make an adequate Olympic Village? Remember, the athletes will be there for two weeks. In the space below, design such a village with facilities for athletes from all participating countries. (Don't forget kitchens capable of supplying different ethnic foods, etc.)

4. Read more about Luz Long, the German long jumper. Complete a trading card form (page 4) with information.

5. Explain/discuss racial prejudice and white supremacy as it affects life in the United States today.

6. Write a report about the political changes in Berlin since 1936.

Olympic Village Design

Babe Didrikson Zaharias

(1914–1956)

Mildred Ella Didrikson was born on June 26, 1914, in Port Arthur, Texas. Her parents were Norwegian immigrants. Her father was a furniture refinisher, and her mother worked as a housekeeper. The family of seven children had little money, but they enjoyed active lives playing on exercise equipment built by their father. It was from this beginning that Babe developed her interest in sports. While still a junior high school student, she determined she would be the greatest athlete who ever lived.

Her career in sports began with the Golden Cyclone Athletic Club, a women's amateur basketball team sponsored by the Employers Casualty Company in Dallas, Texas. She worked as a secretary in order to compete on their basketball and track teams. In 1932 Babe entered the National Amateur Athletic Union (AAU) as a one–woman team representing the Employers Casualty Company. She scored 30 points in eight events, winning the meet by herself against teams of two dozen people. She was permitted to enter only three events in the 1932 Olympics. Babe chose the javelin, hurdles, and high jump. She won two gold medals (with world record performances) and a silver medal in the high jump.

After the Olympics, she was a star and toured the country playing basketball and softball on men's teams. She became interested in golf and won her first tournament in 1934. Babe seemed to excel at any sport she tried. She could pass a football 50 yards and was able to hit home runs off major league pitchers. She also participated in harness racing, billiards, soccer, and skating.

In 1938 she married George Zaharias, a wrestler who gave up his career to coach her. Babe dominated women's golf from 1940–1950, winning 82 amateur and professional golf tournaments all over the world. Babe was named Woman Athlete of the Year six times between 1945 and 1954, and in 1950 was named the Outstanding Female Athlete of the First Half-Century by the Associated Press. She was stricken with cancer and died September 27, 1956.

Suggested Activities and Extensions

1. Babe Didrikson Zaharias was successful at several different sports. Make graphs to show your students' preferences in sports to see and play.

2. Assign brief reports about each sport (harness racing, baseball, billiards, boxing, basketball, football, etc.) in which Babe Didrikson excelled. Compile a class book with the information.

3. Babe Didrikson was a founder and charter member of the Ladies Professional Golf Association (LPGA). Write for more information about her contribution to women's golf:

   > Ladies Professional Golf Association
   > 2570 W. International Speedway Blvd., Suite B
   > Daytona Beach, Florida 32114

4. In 1929, Babe set the women's world record javelin throw with a distance of 133' 3¹/₄". The javelin is a spear made of wood or metal with a pointed steel tip. It weighs 1¹/₂ pounds and is about 7¹/₂ feet long. Estimate a distance of 133 feet and discuss the science of making such a throw. Babe was just 5' 4", 105 pounds at the time. If you wish, select students who are about that size and provide them with a 1¹/₂ pound weight. They should sprint to a foul line and throw the weight as far as possible. Compare the distance to Babe's record throw.

5. Write/Discuss:
   - What opportunities might Babe have had if she had been born later (e.g., after the women's rights movement)?
   - Do you believe Babe would have received greater recognition if she had been a male athlete?
   - What else might she have accomplished if she had lived to an old age?
   - Research to see whether any other woman golfer has won as many titles as Babe Didrikson did.

6. Babe Didrikson was born in Port Arthur, Texas, a city on the Gulf of Mexico. Locate Port Arthur on a map. Prepare an enlarged display (poster, map, list of geographical and industrial facts) of this area. Include information on the following matters:
   - main industries
   - present population
   - nearby cities
   - major river(s)
   - climate conditions (humidity; frequency of storms, hurricanes, tornados, and rainfall; prevailing temperature ranges, etc.)
   - major wildlife native to the area (from alligators and armadillos to roseate spoonbills)

Related Reading

Babe Didrikson, Athlete of the Century by R.R. Knudson. Viking, 1985.

The Sports Career of Mildred Didrikson Zaharias by James Hahn and Lynn Hahn. Crestwood, 1981.

Babe and Jim

Babe Didrikson Zaharias was named the Female Athlete of the First Half-Century by the Associated Press, the women's equivalent to an honor also given Jim Thorpe. Read the biography sheets of these two athletes. Think about similarities and differences between them. Summarize your ideas in the Venn diagram below.

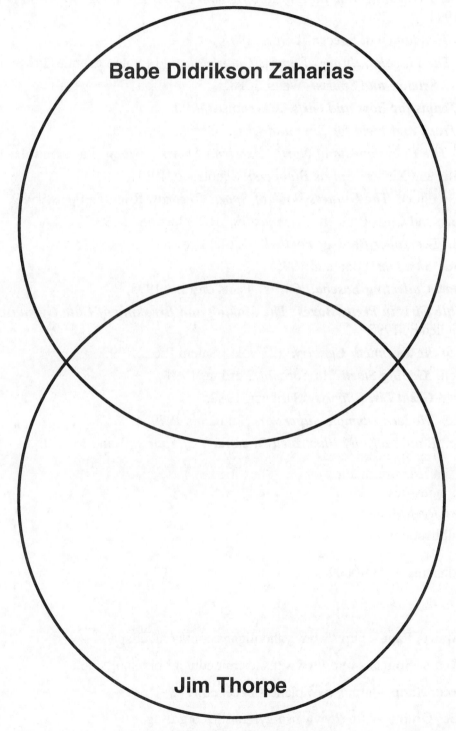

Answer the following question on the back of this paper: Who do you think might be the Male and Female Athletes for the Second Half of the Century? Explain the reasons for your selections.

Bibliography

Aanseng, Nathan. *Comeback Stars of Pro Sports.* Lerner, 1983.

Aanseng, Nathan. *Winners Never Quit: Athletes Who Beat the Odds.* Lerner, 1980.

Bennett, Frank. *The Illustrated Rules of Basketball.* Ideal Books for Children, 1994.

Benson, Michael. *Dream Teams.* Little, Brown, 1991.

Braden, Vic and Louis Phillips. *Sportsathon.* Puffin, 1986.

Cohen, Neil. *The Everything You Want to Know About Sports Encyclopedia.* Sports Illustrated for Kids Book, 1994.

Coleman, Lori. *Fundamental Soccer.* Lerner, 1995.

Frontier Press. *The Lincoln Library of Sports Champions.* (14 vols.) Frontier Press, 1993.

Gardner, Robert. *Science and Sports.* Watts, 1988.

Gutman, Bill. *Tennis for Boys and Girls.* Cavendish, 1990.

Gutman, Bill. *Track and Field for Boys and Girls.* Cavendish, 1990.

Hickok, Ralph. *The Encyclopedia of North American Sports History.* Facts on File, 1992.

Hollander, Phyllis and Xavier. *Sports Bloopers.* Scholastic, 1991.

Krebs, Gary M. (editor). *The Guiness Book of Sports Records.* Running Press, 1989.

McSweeney, Sean and Chris Bunnett. *Gymnastics.* B.T. Batsford, 1993.

Miller, J. David. *The Super Book of Football.* Little, Brown, 1990.

Packard, Edward. *Sky-Jam!* Bantam, 1995.

Plaut, Dave. *Start Collecting Baseball Cards.* Facts on File, 1995.

Ryan, Joan. *Little Girls in Pretty Boxes: The Making and Breaking of Elite Gymnasts and Figure Skaters.* Doubleday, 1995.

Great Athletes of the Twentieth Century. (23 vols.) Salem Press, 1992.

Strachan, Gordon. *Getting Started in Soccer.* Sterling, 1994.

Sullivan, George. *Great Lives-Sports.* Scribner, 1988.

Sullivan, George. *Modern Olympic Superstars.* Putnam's 1979.

Wright, Graeme. *Rand McNally Illustrated Dictionary of Sports.* Rand McNally, 1978.

Periodical

Sports Illustrated for Kids

Time Warner Publications

Box 830609

Birmingham, Alabama 35283-0609

Web Sites

Yahooligans! Sports Page—http://www.yahooligans.com/content/spa/

World Wide Web of Sports—http://www.tns.lcs.mit.edu/cgi-bin/sports/nba

The Planet Soccer Shop—http://www.planet-soccer.com/

USA Gymnastics Online—http://www.usa-gymnastics.org/usag